Raider sat at the table and waited, eyeing the seven men. He smiled to himself knowingly as he saw them quiet and put their glasses on the bar . . .

The silk shawl over Raider's right hand jumped as the bullet swept out of its folds.

"Ah, Raider!" said Doc as he walked in with Adele on his arm and spied the dead men: "I see you've been at it again!"

J.D. HARDIN

BOUNTY
HUNTER

BERKLEY BOOKS, NEW YORK

BOUNTY HUNTER

A Berkley Book / published by arrangement with
the author

PRINTING HISTORY
Berkley edition / December 1983

ISBN: 0-425-06412-3

A BERKLEY BOOK ® TM 757,375
Berkley Books are published by The Berkley Publishing Group,
200 Madison Avenue, New York, N.Y. 10016.
The name "BERKLEY" and the stylized "B" with design are trademarks
belonging to Berkley Publishing Corporation.

PRINTED IN THE UNITED STATES OF AMERICA

CHAPTER ONE

Two well-dressed men in derbies strolled down a street in Amarillo, in the Panhandle of Texas. Although both were handsome and perfectly groomed, there was one essential difference between them—one had a short chain connecting his manacled wrists and the other had papers identifying himself as a Pinkerton agent. They were on their way to the marshal's office.

"I told you I'd get him," the Pinkerton agent announced as they went through the doorway.

"Doc Weatherbee," the marshal greeted him. He motioned to a deputy to lead the manacled man away to a cell as Doc released him. "You got him with the goods?"

Doc pulled out a sheaf of stock certificates from an inside pocket. "Forty thousand dollars worth at face value and not a genuine one among them."

The marshal examined the certificates. "Beautiful workmanship, you've got to grant him that. How can you be sure they're forgeries?"

1

"I couldn't," Doc said, "so I telegraphed the serial numbers in before I set out with him for Amarillo. I got the answer yesterday. These are all fakes."

"They'll be expecting him, then. I'll hold him in the town jail till I get someone to escort him. You going to be staying in town a while, Doc?"

"I hope so. But now that the agency knows I've completed my assignment, I expect they'll have something new for me real soon."

The marshal laughed. "Allan Pinkerton is a thrifty Scot. It pains him to have to pay an idle man."

"I give him little pain on that score. I could use a few free days."

"A lawman's work is never done," the marshal said with a smile.

Doc Weatherbee took himself down to the telegraph office. He had a feeling his next assignment might already have been sent to him. Sure enough, a telegram awaited him. He unfolded the sheet of paper with its heading "The Western Union Telegraph Company" and read the clerk's handwriting.

Three West Texas banks and the Missouri, Kansas, and Texas Railroad have jointly employed the services of the Pinkerton National Detective Agency to capture, dead or alive, one Joseph Fields on multiple charges of murder, rape, kidnapping, and robbery. Proceed at once to Williamville on the Pecos River, where you will be joined by Raider.   Wagner

It had not taken them long to put him back on the job. He looked forward to working again with Raider, his longtime partner on many assignments. He and Raider had very different personalities, but instead of this causing a clash between them, it actually helped them.

Doc Weatherbee left the telegraph office. He had a lot of arrangements to make and was going over them in his mind as he walked down the street. Yet this did not cause him to miss the two men who turned down the empty alley after him. At a glance, they seemed to be cowhands and a bit drunk. Both wore revolvers. Doc figured they had been living it up on the town, that gamblers and women had cleaned them out and they weren't ready yet to go back on the ranges to sweat an honest dollar. He knew how he looked to them. His gray curled-brim derby, his eastern-style gray suit, his silk shirt and vest—these all meant only one thing in their eyes: money.

The two men were about ten paces behind him and gaining on him fast when Doc whirled about to face them. The two men's right hands dropped to their gun handles, but they didn't draw when they saw that Doc's gun hand was empty. Yet both were aware that this stranger could have gotten the drop on them but hadn't bothered.

Doc smiled in a friendly way. "I wouldn't want you boys to make a terrible mistake. In a big town like this, full of strangers, sometimes you can pick on the wrong man."

He flashed them another smile, turned on his heel, and continued down the alley.

One of the cowhands looked back over his shoulder, then up at the flat roofs. He couldn't see anyone who might be covering this man. They looked at Doc walking unhurriedly away.

They didn't know Doc was unarmed and alone.

One shook his head at the other. "Let's try someone else."

They called him Crazy Joe. That was fine with him. He'd show them he could live up to the name they put on him. Joe Fields sat in the saddle of a big bay gelding and looked down into the valley, where a line of smoke rose from the chimney of a lone ranch house. The woman would be cooking. Pangs of hunger stabbed his belly— hunger for cooked food, hunger for a woman.

His restless blue eyes took in the rest of the valley. No sign of men working, no horses hitched on the rail outside the bunkhouse, only a few unsaddled horses in the corral. The men must be out on the range somewhere. From his vantage point on the steep side of the valley, he could see that it would be an hour's ride for any horseman to get to the ranch house. He himself was twenty minutes away. He would have all the time he needed. Crazy Joe Fields could get a lot done in forty minutes. Spurring the bay gelding forward, he descended through the oaks that concealed his advance till he reached the floor of the valley.

Now he smelled the smoke of the wood fire, and the thought of hot food made his mouth water and drool down his unshaven chin, like a wolf slavering over his prey. Life alone in the mountains took its toll on a man, made his rough ways savage and wild, repellent to his fellow human beings. Joe reckoned that was why they called him crazy. Though it might also have something to do with the things he had done to people.

Crazy Joe dismounted and tied his horse out of sight among the trees. Keeping the bunkhouse between him and the ranch house, he approached on foot. The bunkhouse was empty. He didn't bother to go through the men's belongings, since he knew only too well how poorly cowhands were paid and how they blew every penny on payday in the closest town. The ranch house door was open, and some chickens pecked in the ground before it.

The woman was bent over the table near the stove, chopping vegetables with a big kitchen knife. His nostrils filled with the aroma of a stew simmering in a pot, and his eyes wandered over the shapely backside of the woman in the prairie dress bent over her task and unaware of his presence. The only sound was the chop, chop, chop of her knife on the vegetables.

"Got a plate of food for a hungry stranger, ma'am?"

Her body froze at the sound of his voice. Slowly she turned around to face him. He noticed she was still gripping the knife.

"I could use a bite to eat, ma'am. I'll pay for it if you want."

"Where did you come from?" the woman asked in an unsteady voice.

She had gotten over her initial shock at the presence of an intruder in her house, but was plainly not much relieved now that she had had a chance to examine his appearance. His denims were bleached from sun and wear, his hat was greasy and stained with sweat, his mouth was straight and almost lipless over his long yellowed teeth, his bright blue eyes had an uncaring, unreasoning brilliance.

The woman knew she had not managed to conceal the look of dislike on her face, but she had hidden the fear, the panic, that had gripped her. She lived in a man's world and fed daily the rowdies and drifters her husband con-

stantly had to hire to help his regular men on the ranch.
Both she and Crazy Joe were aware of the long sharp blade
she held between them, and also of the .45 revolver slung
on his left hip.

"My husband will be mad as hell if he finds you in
here. We don't want your money. Wait outside and I'll
bring a plate of stew out to you."

He made no move, just stood there looking at her as if
he couldn't understand a word she was saying.

"Go on, git," she told him. "I'll bring your food out to
you."

"I ain't leaving here, lady, till I get what I came for."

"No one's asking you to leave. I said wait outside."

"I kind of enjoy having a roof over my head once in a
while," he said. "You quit ordering me around and hustle
up some food. A man like me don't care to be kept
waiting."

He caught the strange look that came to her eyes and the
suddenly willing way she went to the stove, and he was
instantly on guard.

She stirred the stew. "It'll be ready in a moment."

Crazy Joe was hit from behind, with two feet in the
small of his back, and thrust forward to his hands and
knees on the floor. He looked up and saw a short Chinese
man with a pigtail regain his balance and run toward him,
aiming a kick at his head. Joe ducked and his left hand
slithered down over the handle of his gun.

The kick passed harmlessly over his head as he pulled
the revolver from its holster, cocked and aimed it, then
pulled the trigger. The gun spoke as the Chinese turned to
strike at him with the edge of a flattened hand, and the
.45-caliber bullet brushed the man's light body away like a
hand slapping a fly.

The woman came at him, standing over him where he lay and holding her knife in both hands to drive the blade down into his body with all her strength. Crazy Joe pointed the barrel of his .45 upward and caught her with a bullet between the breasts. Her soft warm body capsized on top of him and the knife clattered on the floor beside his head.

He pushed her off him and got to his feet. Having searched the other rooms in the house, he returned to the kitchen and ladled stew onto a plate. He sat down at the table next to the two bodies and spooned the food into his mouth. It was venison, carrots, potatoes, and onions, and he ate four platefuls before he was satisfied. A pity he had killed the woman, he thought. She would have provided him with some pleasure. That damned little Chinese with his flying kick had nearly done for him. He had been careless. That sort of carelessness could spell the end for him.

Crazy Joe looked through the house again, more carefully this time, opening closets and drawers. They would have gold coins hidden away—but he would never find them in a short time. He thought he might come across some money used to pay the men and buy supplies. He found nothing. Pity she was dead—he could have forced her to tell him the whereabouts of the money. He saw nothing of any value to him and returned to the kitchen. Looking out the open door, he scanned the valley for a sign of anyone approaching. Nothing.

He went back inside and kicked the body of the Chinese man. It flopped over lifelessly. Then he stooped and touched the cheek of the dead woman. Her body was still warm. Damn, he thought, he had never humped a dead woman before. But he had raped them when they were so terror-stricken their limbs locked and couldn't move, and he had hit others on the head when they had tried to bite or scratch him. So it might not make all that much difference. He looked down at the graceful body at his feet. A real pity he had killed her so soon. He began to unbutton his fly.

Raider opened the telegram and read it, peeling away the shirt stuck to his back with sweat. If it was hot here in the Indian Territory, it was going to be a lot hotter down in the southwest of Texas just above the border. Williamville on the Pecos River. Must be a small cattle town.

Doc Weatherbee would be there. Raider could use the change of working with a real professional whose reactions he could depend upon, after the two agents who had been with him in the Indian Territory. Both had held down desk jobs in the Chicago office of the Pinkerton National Detective Agency and realized that they needed what they called "experience in the field" before they could be promoted up the bureaucratic ladder. They had decided they could choose no better place to look for action than the Indian Territory. In practice there was almost no law enforcement there and little government. Then they had chosen the legendary Raider to guarantee them a lot of experience in a short time. They intended to get back to their desk jobs as soon as possible and get on with the realities of life, such as promotions and higher salaries.

The only trouble was that they had meant to go along as onlookers, as tourists, while Raider took pleasure in endangering their lives by exposing them to risky situations and leaving it up to them to figure a way out. From Raider's point of view, all he was doing was letting these two ambitious types, who undoubtedly would end up as managers and bosses, see what life was really like for an agent. Maybe at some future date they would give a little thought to the men they sent on assignments from the safety of the four walls of their office. Both had survived their ordeal in the Indian Territory. Raider guessed it would be a long time before they bothered him again.

They had seen action. The band of outlaws the three Pinkerton agents were tracking had made the mistake of trying a surprise attack on a settlement of Kiowa Indians to steal food, fresh horses, ammunition, and whatever else they could lay their hands on. Like other Indians in the territory, the Kiowas had been left without protection to the depredations of white outlaws and with no recourse to the law. It usually was a mistake to attack someone who expected the worst and was prepared for it. The Kiowas wiped out the outlaws—and very nearly also the two Pinkerton agents placed in Raider's charge. Or so both Raider and the Kiowas had led them to believe. Those Indians had a sense of humor, and those two office workers from Chicago were a joke.

Now Raider had a long journey ahead of him, from one corner of Texas to the opposite one. What he needed right away was a good meal. In an eating house he was served a plate of sliced mutton, boiled potatoes, and gravy. He paid for it and took his change. Then it occurred to him he had been shortchanged. The meal was a quarter, and he had gotten back only three quarters from a five-dollar gold piece.

"You gave me a silver dollar," the bleary-eyed man behind the counter claimed, "not five dollars."

Raider eyed him. "I had that gold piece in my vest pocket here, and it ain't here now, so I know I gave it to you."

The counterman warily surveyed Raider. He saw a big man with a tanned, tough face that sported a black mustache curving gracefully down from his nostrils and turned sharply inward at the corners of his mouth. A scuffed black leather jacket made his broad shoulders look even broader than they were. His blue denim pants and black calfskin Middleton boots were as battered as his leather jacket. He had a black Stetson on his head and a .44 Remington on his hip. The revolver looked a lot better cared for than his clothes. It looked clean, oiled, and ready to move.

"Listen, mister," the counterman said, "you're making a mistake. I don't cheat no one in this place. I serve them good food and charge reasonable prices."

"You owe me four dollars," Raider said quietly.

The counterman took in his accuser's easy gunfighter's stance and decided not to make an issue of it. He paid out four silver dollars, and Raider took them and returned to his food. The meal was good. He searched in his vest pockets for a nickel to leave under his plate and found the five-dollar gold piece.

Raider grinned. The counterman had been right after all and had been frightened into shelling out four dollars to him. He tucked the gold piece under the plate edge as a tip.

Charles Harker was the fourth of five sons of an Illinois farmer. There would be no land coming to him when old man Harker died, and Charles, from the time he was sixteen on, knew exactly what he wanted: the middle Nolan girl and a spread of his own not too far from his pa's in the fertile land of Illinois. She had said she would wait for him, and he knew he was going back someday to Illinois.

He had gone first to Mexico in search of gold and silver, but found he was twenty years too late. Only two days south of El Paso, he and his companions were robbed and beaten by bandits. One died on the walk back across the blistering sands to the border.

But Charles had not given up his hope of raising fast money to buy his own spread and enjoy it while he was still a young man. He had been four years on his own now, had turned twenty, and at last had found a source of big money—bounty hunting. It was a lot more risky than mining, but then that was why it paid good. Charles liked to say to people who warned him, a man don't reap if he don't risk.

He had started out with shooting Mexican sheep stealers at fifty dollars a head. At first he had been sympathetic. He had listened to the thieves' stories and had even let some go. He had taken them alive and had been shocked when the ranchers strung them up when he brought them in. It was more merciful for him to kill them with a quick bullet. They were often hard to catch in the act of stealing, so he started shooting some who he knew without doubt were on their way to steal—and in a while extended that to anyone who looked as if they might steal sheep. Finally he just shot any Mexicans he found on the sheep ranges and collected fifty dollars per head on them.

Cattle rustlers paid more. However, they were usually well armed and operated in gangs. Charles developed a method of bagging them. He tracked them to where they were rounding up a herd, waited until they had the herd on the move, until every man of them was riding hard to cut off strays and keep the animals together. With his Winchester rifle, he always managed to pick off one—and sometimes two or even three—of the rustlers. Even when the others saw him, they were never willing to abandon the herd in order to come after him.

When the rustlers and the herd had gone, all Charles had to do was ride in and finish off the downed rustler, bring his body back, and collect the bounty on him. He wished luck to the rustlers who had gotten away, since the more cattle stolen in an area, the higher the bounties.

Then he heard of the $5,000 reward on Crazy Joe Fields. With that money and what he had already saved, he could ride north right away, buy a big spread, and collect the Nolan girl.

He knew how dangerous Crazy Joe was supposed to be, but this opportunity was too good to miss. Crazy Joe was a windfall. Charles would be careful. Very careful.

Crazy Joe had been seen only a few days previously out by Natchez Ridge, a long spine of red rock with the only freshwater springs in a hundred square miles. Harker knew the area because cattle liked to gather near the springs and its remoteness made it ideal for rustlers. He rode out early in the morning, and at midday he was lying facedown in the sand with his horse's reins caught under his body. Man and animal were in full view of anyone on Natchez Ridge who had come for water.

The sun beat down and fried him for a solid three hours, and his horse snorted and repeatedly tried to free the reins as it gasped through its open mouth. The reins were tied to

Harker's left leg, and the horse was going nowhere. Harker needed him there. A standing horse was a lot easier to notice than a fallen man.

Harker was almost at the point of deciding he might die for real if he stayed out in the sun like this for much longer when he spotted a horseman approaching, peering from beneath the brim of his hat. He waited. The horse and its rider were coming nearer slowly and warily, almost at a walk. This had to be Joe Fields. If it wasn't, he'd hide the body and try something else. As the horse drew closer, Charles Harker's hand reached beneath him for the rifle he was lying on.

He pushed the rifle out on the dry earth before him, keeping the muzzle raised an inch so that no soil got into the barrel. He looked along the sights and drew a bead on the horseman. This wasn't easy to do, because he found now that his exposure to the heat had affected his vision, making images wavery and jumpy. He steadied himself, stared hard to clear his vision, and squeezed the trigger. The horseman stiffened, clung a moment in the saddle, and fell to the ground beside his horse.

Having jumped to his feet in triumph, Harker now felt dizzy. He steadied himself against his horse and then ran forward to the man he had knocked from the saddle. He wanted to see his face. He knew what Crazy Joe looked like from the WANTED posters. This could be his ticket back to a good life in Illinois. He would leave the very day he collected the bounty.

It was Crazy Joe Fields without a doubt who lay there on his back beside his bewildered horse. Charles had got him! Charles stood over his prize and noticed too late that the man's holster was empty. Next thing he knew, he was looking down into a pair of bright blue eyes and into the one dark eye of the gun barrel in Joe's left hand.

Charles Harker saw the flame spit up at him and felt a terrible pain in his gut that spread everywhere in his body, out to the knuckles of his fingers, to the bones of his feet. He was lying now on the dusty soil, and Texas was fading fast before his eyes. . . . Charles knew where he was going. . . . At last! Home to Illinois . . .

CHAPTER TWO

Joe Fields could not swim, and clung by his horse's side to the saddle as the animal made its way across the Pecos River. The Pecos was not wide, but it was a bigger river than it looked, running deep, swift, red, and muddy. Its violent currents bore the animal downstream as it swam across, and by the time it found footing in shallow water on the far side, horse and rider were a quarter mile down from where they had started.

Crazy Joe let the horse rest, drink, and graze. He dried his clothes in the early morning sun. West of the Pecos, water was scarce. Bone dry and hard going. He could not stop long, since he had to make time before the sun got high.

Having ridden for some hours west of the river, he came to foothills gouged by canyons. The huge red rocks had a scant covering of vegetation, on which some beat-up sheep were grazing. Around a shoulder of rock, he saw an adobe house with children playing in its shade. He slowed his horse to a walk and held the reins high so that whoever was in the house could see he had no gun in his hands.

A Mexican came out of the dark doorway of the house, dressed in a white loose-fitting shirt and pants, sandals, and a sombrero. He cradled a rifle in his arms, courteously pointing its barrel away from the newcomer. His wife emerged behind him and began to gather her children.

Crazy Joe stopped his horse a hundred yards away, beyond accurate pistol range—again a gesture of goodwill. "You know who I am?"

"*Sí, señor,*" the Mexican called back.

"I'm looking for El Caballito del Diablo. You seen him recently?"

"*Sí.* He speaks well of you."

Crazy Joe moved his horse forward again and continued his slow pace up to the front of the house. He remembered his manners and tipped his hat to the lady.

"*Buenas días, señora.* You have fine children." He looked down at the five little faces topped with jet black hair and whose dark eyes gazed up at him unwaveringly. "You know who I am, *muchachos*? Loco Jose, I suppose you'd call me."

"Crazy Joe," the less shy of the children chorused.

He rolled his blue eyes, which made them laugh.

"Come inside, señor," the man said, "you will eat with us, and I have corn and water for your horse. My name is Ignacio Sanchez."

Inside the adobe house it was dark and cool. They ate tortillas filled with sheep's cheese spiced with peppers. After the meal, the woman cleared the table and the children went outside to play. The hottest part of the day would soon be over, and Crazy Joe told his host that he would soon be on his way. Sanchez poured two glasses of tequila.

He held up his glass. "To a difficult life, señor."

"Sure." Fields threw back his drink in a single gulp. He hated the taste of tequila but enjoyed the belt of alcohol.

"I understand El Caballito," the Mexican was saying. "His Comanche people belonged to these parts before the Washington government shipped them to the Indian Territory. It is natural for him to want to return to the place of his birth, even if he has to live there like a coyote in the hills. But your position is not like that, señor. You could go to California or Nevada or anyplace where you are not known and there start a new life. Yet you remain around here, where you are hunted and cursed. Forgive my curiosity, señor, but this is a great mystery to me."

Joe Fields accepted another glass of tequila. He looked the Mexican over. The man made no effort to hide his recognition of the fact that he and his family survived out here at the mercy of bandits and renegades. He was not worth stealing from, and this provided him with a sort of protection. Yet he entertained with a self-mocking sense of style, as if he were a great *ranchero* at his hacienda. He even had the courage to put questions that had no easy answers. Fields found the man's lack of fear of him and lack of threat to him something new.

"Why do I stay around here?" Crazy Joe posed the question to himself. "I guess it's because I know the country, for one thing. That's a big thing in a man's favor."

The Mexican nodded in agreement.

Joe went on, "And maybe I seen enough here and don't

want to start all over again in a new place. I ain't goin' to change, even if the place does.''

Sanchez muttered something in Spanish, of which Fields understood only something about "a man's fate." He knew Mexicans. In no time at all the man would be rambling on about death and life and man's brief stay on this bitter earth. Joe had no use for this kind of talk. You went out and did things, in his opinion. You did not sit and allow things to be done to you.

"When do you expect to see El Caballito del Diablo again?"

"*Quién sabe?*"

"Where did he go?"

The Mexican only smiled.

Something caught Crazy Joe's eye. He stared out through the open doorway, then he grabbed the Mexican's rifle from where it leaned against a wall. He brought the gun to his shoulder swiftly and took aim, while Sanchez jumped to his feet to see what Crazy Joe was firing at. To his horror, he saw his three-year-old son Diego standing there alone. This was the target of the crazy gringo! He whipped out a knife and went for Crazy Joe's throat. Too late. The rifle cracked, and the gunman pulled his head away from the knife thrust.

The Mexican held the point of the blade to Joe's right carotid artery and fearfully glanced out the door. He saw his child running toward him.

"You missed!" he joyfully spat at Crazy Joe.

Joe Fields ignored the blade at his throat and put the rifle on the table. "No, I didn't miss."

The Mexican looked again.

The body of a headless three-foot rattler squirmed on the ground near where his son had stood.

• • •

"Naw, he don't come into town anymore," the clerk at the Hotel Williamville told Raider. "Nor any other town hereabouts neither. Folks would put a quick end to Crazy Joe Fields if he showed his face in Williamville."

"Plus the fact there's five thousand on his head," Raider observed.

The clerk grinned. "You bet. A man don't keep too many loyal friends if he's worth that much dead or alive."

"That's the whole idea."

The garrulous clerk continued, "That wasn't always the case though. Crazy Joe used to stay right here in this hotel all the times he was in town. That's when he was wanted by the law in some places, I guess, but there was no reward on his head and he was no worse than two score other gunslingers in this town."

"He's fast with his gun?" Raider inquired.

"Like lightning. And he had a good head on his shoulders too, before he started to act strange. He could add up ten different amounts in his head and give you the answer before you properly got ink on your pen to figure it on paper. Then he started to behave moody, and he'd look through you like you wasn't there one minute and clap you on the back and say hello the next minute. You could never tell where you were with him. Some days he would sit in the dining room talking to the food as he was eating it. No one interrupted him neither. Or dared laugh so he could see them. Though I don't think he much cared what people thought of him."

"You seem to have liked him," Raider said.

"Sure. I got nothing against Joe."

"Then why are you telling me this when you know I'm a bounty hunter looking to bring him in?" Raider asked.

The clerk grinned. "I told some other bounty hunters exactly what I'm telling you. I don't think I was much help to them, because they ain't around no more."

"Joe got them?"

"I expect so," the clerk said.

Raider had arrived in Williamville before Doc Weatherbee. On his first night there he had heard of the reward for Crazy Joe, which had remained uncollected for eight months now. Neither Doc nor Raider could claim the five thousand if they were successful, because they were Pinkerton agents hired out by the same people who had offered the reward. Raider saw that the easiest way for him to get information on Joe Fields was to pretend to be a drifter who had just heard of some easy money to be made by collecting the bounty.

Giving advice on how to collect the bounty on Fields had become a local pastime. Raider saw that most of the ones doing the talking had no intention of putting their lives on the line by actually going in pursuit of the outlaw. Too cowardly to go themselves, they resented those who did. Thus their advice was suspect.

The one word Raider never mentioned in relation to himself was "Pinkerton." The Pinkerton National Detective Agency had made a lot of enemies, and for men who waited with grudges to settle, one Pinkerton agent was as good as another. Raider had no wish to take a bullet in the back for some wrong, real or imagined, that another agent had done—though he reckoned most of the grudges were based on resentment of fair captures and the punishment that followed. While he was just another body floating into town, Raider could learn more and operate with greater freedom than any known Pinkerton agent.

The Hotel Williamville was the best of three hotels in

the town. Of the two others, one was a ramshackle warren of drunken gunmen and the other a bedding stable for the cheapest whores in the saloons. So the Hotel Williamville didn't have a lot of competition.

Doc Weatherbee inquired from a vaquero in a large sombrero if the town ahead was Williamville. It was. He flicked the reins on the rump of his mule, and the wagon moved forward slowly over the uneven trail. Williamville sure didn't look like much of a town, but just the sort of place in need of a traveling doctor. Canvas banners hung on both sides of the rig: DOCTOR WEATHERBEE—HOMEO-PATHIC MEDICINES. FREE CONSULTATION. On board were loaded variously shaped bottles of livid hues, boxes of pills, packages of powders, dried herbs, pamphlets. Cures, balms, salves, tonics. For tired livers. Lower back pain. Nerves. Tired blood. Vapors. All the ills that flesh is heir to.

Doc had purchased the Studebaker wagon, complete with its stock of patent medicines, restorers, and invigorators, from a physician in Carson City. He had seen immediately what a great cover this would provide him for his activities as a Pinkerton agent. At first he had not taken the role seriously, particularly such items as the English remedy that claimed to cure "loss of memory, lassitude, nocturnal emissions, noises in the head, dimness of vision, and aversion to society." However, gradually he had found the role of healer being thrust upon him. Doc went so far as to make sure that all his medicines could cause no one any harm, and working on the basis that most ills are imaginary, he prescribed solemnly and charged accordingly—with excellent results in most cases. When he came across genuine illness, he steered the unfortunates to genuine physicians with qualifications, who likely as not recommended the same harmless items he himself sold. Yet Doc was careful never to mislead a truly sick person.

Judith, Doc's mule, pulled the wagon onward at her relaxed pace. For a long time now, Doc had learned to let Judith have her own way. He had grown very fond of her, and she in turn was not too stubborn so long as things were done the way she wanted them. Now that she had spotted the town ahead, she knew there would be water and oats for her and she needed no urging.

Doc checked the floorboards beneath his medical merchandise to make sure the boards that opened were properly latched. Concealed beneath those boards lay some equipment that was not in the regular stock of a traveling physician: a telegraph key, wires and battery, a pair of Gatling guns that could shoot six hundred rounds per minute, dynamite, and a small arsenal of other weapons and ammunition.

Having raised his derby politely to two horsemen riding out of town, Doc tried to interest them in medicine. The two sneered at him. One spat, and they rode on.

"Maybe we should have asked that quack if he'd seen Crazy Joe," one of the two riders leaving town said after a while.

"Naw. If Joe Fields rode in this close to Williamville— and we got two separate eyewitnesses who saw him only a short while ago—it wasn't to rob some snake-oil doctor. He could have got him out in the backcountry far from town."

"I reckon. What do you think Crazy Joe is doing? Planning on coming into town?"

The second horseman shook his head. "He wouldn't

chance that. He knows there's always the likes of you and me just waiting for him to show his face.''

"Those other fellas who went out after Fields, they were alone?''

"Sure. Went out one by one. They was greedy. Wanted the whole reward to theirself. Us, we're smart. Pitching in together like this, half and half on the bounty, looking out for one another. Crazy Joe don't stand a chance against us.''

"So long as we can trust one another.''

The other rider laughed harshly. "We ain't got no choice but trust each other. Unless you want us both dead.''

They rode on for a while, looking around them for any movement in the thorny scrub or for fresh horse tracks leading away from the rutted trail over the smooth gray soil. They were gaunt, hungry-looking individuals, in their early twenties, with the wary nervous movements of those who lived by their wits.

The one who had some doubts about their partnership said, "You be the one to approach him. I be the backup.''

"Whatever you want.''

"I still don't see how you expect us to run into him out here in the mesquite.''

His partner said patiently, "Crazy Joe let those two see him out this way so they could bring word into town he was out here, It was his way of letting someone in town know he wanted to see him.''

"You don't know who?''

"Hell, no, and I don't care. We were just lucky to be one of the first to hear the news Joe was here. Another hour, the whole town will know, and you'll have a dozen guns out here trying their luck.''

"Then Joe will be watching the trail for whoever it is he wants to meet."

"He may already have met him and been long gone."

"Or he's in one of those thorn thickets right now, looking down a rifle barrel at us."

His partner laughed. "Could be."

They were not far wrong.

At a bend in the trail a little ways on, Joe Fields stepped out from behind a patch of prickly pears. He was about fifty yards from them and held a short-barrel rifle loosely aimed in their direction. Chances were he could get both of them if they went for their guns.

"You boys looking for anyone in particular?" Crazy Joe inquired, his clear blue eyes cold and sharp as those of an eagle.

"What's it to you, stranger?"

"Thought you might be looking for me," Crazy Joe told him.

"Then you was mistaken."

Joe smiled disbelievingly. "You boys been long in Williamville?"

"A few days."

"Ever hear of Fred Denton?"

Both riders thought for a moment, and the one doing the talking said, "Not unless he was the one those Texas Rangers killed in town a couple of days back." Crazy Joe was listening quietly, so the rider continued, "I saw the body outside the marshal's office. Big fella with a full beard, had Mexican silverwork in a leather vest, wore a big yellow silk bandanna. That the one?"

"That's him," Crazy Joe said slowly. "Another good man gone . . ."

"What was he good for?"

Joe pulled himself together and grinned. "Just about anything, I guess. Rustling, holdups, barroom fighting, you name it."

"Sounds like he'll be sorely missed."

"Don't matter much after you've gone what folks say or think," Joe said. He stamped his boot on the dust. "It's while you're above ground you've gotta make it count. You two boys aiming on splitting the five thousand?"

The two riders glanced at each other and looked back at him warily. They knew it was useless to say anything.

"Before I came here looking for Fred Denton, I was over the other side of the Pecos trying to find El Caballito del Diablo. You boys heard of him?"

They nodded.

"Couldn't find him." Fields shook his head. "That's always the way—you have something big and you need help on it, then you can't find nobody or they get theirselves killed." Joe looked them over speculatively. "Course you'd each get a lot more than the five thousand you planned to split on catching me."

The rider who had been doing the talking smiled and was silent now, obviously more than half sold on Joe's idea.

The second rider spoke for the first time. "Catching you is legal."

"It's also more dangerous. And, like I said, it don't pay nearly so well."

The second rider went on, "Supposing this big-money thing of yours doesn't work out, you have nothing to lose. But if we two go in on it with you, we could end up on the run like you."

"Not if it goes the way I see it," Joe said. He was not going out of his way to persuade anyone.

"I don't like the sound of it," the second rider told the first.

"So ride back to town and forget it," the first rider snapped.

Without another word, the man swung his horse about, spurred it, and trotted back the way they had come.

Crazy Joe and the remaining rider exchanged a glance. Crazy Joe nodded.

The man riding away looked back over one shoulder and saw his late partner pulling a rifle from his saddle scabbard. He urged his horse into a gallop and crouched low in the saddle over the animal's neck. The departing man now presented only a swerving, fast-moving, small target, yet the rifleman picked him off with the first shot. The man fell sideways from the saddle, and his left boot caught in the stirrup. The frightened horse eased its pace as it dragged its rider's head and shoulders in the dust.

"You're some backshooter," Crazy Joe said admiringly.

"I've had a lot of practice. Where's this job we're going to do?"

" 'Bout two hours away if we cut across country." Joe pointed. "I got my horse in back of this thicket. You ride in front. I'm not letting you back of me."

They pulled down the brims of their hats to shade their eyes from the glaring sun and made their way over the parched earth, in and out of thickets and around impassable clumps of thorny plants, taking it easy for their horses' sake. But even at this walking pace, the flanks of the beasts were streaked with foaming sweat, and they gasped loudly in the heat.

"You sure you know your way?" the rider called back

to Crazy Joe. "We could be lost out here and they wouldn't find our bones till the next century."

"It's a hard, demanding sort of land," Joe said by way of agreement.

"You know where we're at?"

"Sure. I had to take to living out here, and I wouldn't have lasted long if I couldn't tell where I was going."

The rider began to have doubts. Joe's offer had sounded genuine at first. "Why won't you tell me what we're going to rob?"

"In case you get any ideas about shooting me after you know all you need," Joe told him.

"It'd be damn hard for me to shoot you, since you're riding at my back. How do I know you're not going to shoot me?"

"If I was going to, I'd have done so by now," Joe said reasonably. "Besides, I need you alive."

After almost another hour of plodding across the trackless waste beneath the blazing sun, they came to an area of massive thickets with grass growing in their shade. Wild cattle crashed through the undergrowth now and then, and they had to circle a wild pig that stood its ground and threatened to charge the horses. They drank and watered the horses at a tiny creek, wiped the sweat from their eyes, and remounted. No more than a hundred yards on, they found themselves looking into the rifle barrels of three Mexican horsemen in elaborately fringed leather chaps and sombreros.

"There's probably more in the bushes roundabout," Joe warned his companion.

One of the Mexicans spoke rapidly to them in Spanish.

"You know what he's saying?" the rider muttered to Joe. "I don't know their lingo."

"You let me talk to them," Joe said.

The Mexican spoke in Spanish again and wheeled his horse about.

"He wants us to follow him," Joe explained. "Better do as he says. These boys are rustlers from the other side of the Rio Grande. They got nothing to do with us."

The two other Mexicans brought their horses along in the rear. In a little while they came to a large sandy clearing in the thorn scrub. Fifteen men were eating meat which they cut with their knives from large pieces on a spit over a fire. The hide and remains of the butchered carcass of a wild longhorn lay nearby.

Crazy Joe dismounted, walked forward, and shook hands with a fierce-looking *bandido* who had belts of rifle shells crossing on his chest and pearl-handled Colts at his hips. Joe spoke in a low voice with the man. At one point the Mexicans within hearing range turned to stare at Joe's companion, who was still on his horse.

"What did you say about me?" he called to Joe nervously. "Why are they looking at me?"

Joe turned around to face him. "Seems like one of these boys was shot a few days ago. They claimed I did it until I told them yesterday it was someone I knew and I could bring him to them. Sorry I had to hand you over."

The bandit leader began talking to his men in a loud voice and gesticulating.

"What's he saying?" the mounted man asked Joe. His eyes blazed with hatred, but since Joe Fields was his only source of information, he had to keep on talking terms with him.

Joe said, "He's talking about how the Apaches in the old days used to tie a gringo upside down to one of his wagon wheels, light a small fire under his head, and boil his brains till his skull split.''

The mounted man spat and stayed cool. ''I don't see no wagon wheels hereabouts.''

''I'm sure they'll think of something,'' Joe said very seriously.

''I'll bury you yet, you low bastard.''

He slapped his horse and rode into the men, scattering them. None of them tried to shoot him down as he made his escape. This was left to their leader. One of his pearl-handled Colts barked four times, and the bounty hunter slid out of his saddle next to the discarded carcass of the longhorn.

''You want me to believe he was the one who killed Jacinto?'' the leader asked Crazy Joe.

''I didn't kill Jacinto,'' Joe said. ''But I got you this gringo who might have done it. Your men have seen you take your revenge, so you're still *el numero uno grande*. You ought to thank me as a friend.''

The *bandido* bared his sparkling fangs in a smile and put his pistol in its holster. ''*Gracias, amigo.*''

The traveling physician known as Doc Weatherbee and the would-be bounty hunter named Raider met as if by chance in a saloon.

''I saw you arriving in town as I rode out with the others,'' Raider said. ''Know where I was going?''

Doc shook his head.

''Joe Fields had been spotted back along the trail you were on. We found a bounty hunter shot dead and dragging by one foot in his left stirrup just a few miles past where I saw you. Crazy Joe had to have been watching you pass by.''

"Pity he didn't have a toothache or a pain in his gut, he might have stopped me for some medicine. I think I saw the two bounty hunters you're talking about."

"They say two left town. We found only one."

Doc grimaced. "I bet the buzzards or coyotes will find the other."

"You've been hearing stories about Joe Fields?"

"He seems to be one of the main topics of conversation in this town," Doc confirmed.

Raider beckoned to a woman who stood hesitantly at the batwing doors of the saloon. "You're going to see what else I've been doing since I hit town."

Doc was surprised at Raider's acquaintance with this very ladylike woman who was nervously making her way between the saloon tables toward them. She looked as if she would be more comfortable finding her way among the pews of a church. But she was pretty and had a long slender body, Doc granted her that. She was dressed in a long narrow skirt and a severe tunic buttoned up to her chin. Gloves covered her hands, and a veil hung from her hat. She had not left an inch of bare skin exposed.

Doc stood, shook hands with her wordlessly, and took in the surprised look she gave him. The lady was very obviously surprised to find Raider, the roustabout and gunfighter, in the company of this nicely mannered, elegantly clad physician. Doc regarded this as very amusing. She and Raider exchanged polite conversation. Doc appreciated their efforts to include him in their little chat, but his attention was soon distracted by a startlingly beautiful blonde who came in and sat at a table by herself.

"Excuse me," Doc told Raider and his ladylike friend, whose name he had already forgotten. He left their table and approached the blonde. "May I buy you a drink?"

"Sure."

He sat at the table and waved to the waiter. "Some good bourbon all right with you?" he asked her.

"Sure."

She might not be a whole lot conversationally, but she was great to look at. Her long yellow tresses rested on her bare shoulders, above her shimmering green silk gown. A black ribbon bearing a cameo circled her neck. She had a narrow face, full lips, and melting brown eyes. Her breasts swelled, almost bursting from the captivity of her low-cut gown. This was about as much as Doc could see, since she was sitting at the table. They were talking away to each other of things of no consequence, laughing and having a good time, when a heavyset man came to their table and placed a calloused, scarred hand on her shoulder in a proprietary way. She shrugged out from beneath his grasp.

"Adele, I want you to come with me," the man growled.

"I ain't," the blonde replied.

"You're going to, if I have to pick you up and throw you over my shoulder."

"I ain't going," Adele said.

Doc smiled easily at the man. "I'll give you some advice, friend. Better deal with me before you try putting her over your shoulder. She might hinder your fighting style."

The man looked carefully at Doc and noted the confident way he was still relaxed in his chair.

"She ain't worth it," the heavyset man said, and was about to turn away.

"I think she is," Doc told him in a clear voice. "I won't hear you speak ill of this lady."

The man grunted furtively and moved away. The crowd of drinkers at the bar snickered as they always did when a man had to back down from high and mighty behavior because his bluff had been called.

"The Hotel Williamville is across the way," Doc said suggestively to his lovely friend. "We could take this bourbon bottle along with us."

Raider glanced out the saloon window and saw Doc Weatherbee and the blonde enter the hotel lobby opposite. It occurred to Raider there was a lot of horse sense to Doc's choice in women. He himself had quite a ways to go before he could persuade this woman to make a similar trip with him. Raider glanced at her face and discovered she was almost speechless from shock.

"Surely you're not surprised . . ." he said to her, assuming that perhaps Doc's short courtship of the blonde had offended her feminine sensibilities.

"It's not your friend and that slut I object to," she said primly. "It's my boss and that slut that has upset me."

"You mean the heavyset man Doc chased off just now?"

"That's Noah Blake, owner of the Tumbling K Ranch."

"The one whose children you're governess to?" Raider asked sympathetically. For some reason he could never understand, women liked to impose the highest moral standards on the men they worked for. Self-protection, he guessed.

"He has the loveliest wife imaginable and two sweet children," she said indignantly, "and here he is in a nest of vipers quarreling with a stranger over a painted woman."

"Lucky he didn't notice you here," Raider put in.

She flushed. "I have a right to be where I like in my free time."

Raider let that go. He silently cursed his fascination with contrary women and wondered what Doc was up to at that moment.

Doc watched her part her long legs slowly as she lay back naked on the bed, watching him watch her. His hungry eyes traveled over the sensuous curves of her smooth thighs, lingered on her golden skin, on the blond tangle of curls about the pink opening of her sex.

He kicked off his boots while he unbuckled his belt, and then he shucked off his gray suit. His cock jerked rigid at the beautiful woman on the bed, like a water diviner's rod twitching beyond control over some hidden source. She smiled appreciatively at his show of strength and licked her lips invitingly.

Doc kneeled between her thighs and ran his tongue along the silky insides of her legs all the way up to her crotch. Then the tip of his tongue skittered along the shell-pink lips of her vagina, flicked at her clit, darted away, only to suddenly return. He parted her lips with his fingers, exposing the deliciously tender interior of her sex, and dived into it with the full width of his tongue in broad affectionate strokes that caused her to writhe with intense sensation.

His tongue plunged deep within her, and he tasted her juices as he ate her fiercely and her body responded rhythmically to him. He teased her erect clit, sucked it, held it tightly in his compressed lips.

Her fingers caught his hair and pulled his face into the wetness of her cunt as she bucked and cried out in frenzied ecstasy.

CHAPTER THREE

Raider and Doc put in a few days getting to know the lay of the country. Doc went from ranch to ranch, selling his cures and listening to everything anyone had to tell him. Raider rode out to other spreads not visited by Doc, offering his services as a hired gun. While Crazy Joe Fields was all the talk of the town, out on the ranches they cared more about rustlers. Most of the big outfits were willing to take Raider on, paying him either steady wages or a retainer and a bounty on every rustler he nailed. He drifted from one place to the next, as such a gunman would, seeking to find who would pay him most. Between them they got a good idea of the territory they would operate in.

They found it easy to exchange information at the end of the day in casual meetings in saloons. Although they both stayed at the same hotel, they were careful to stay away from each other there, and anywhere else there was not a relaxed feeling of camaraderie.

At one of their short meetings, Raider told Doc, "As

you suggested, I rode off the trail a ways several times today. I spoke to some cowhands at one place. They were looking for some strayed steers, but you could have hidden a whole herd of buffalo in that terrain without being able to spot a single one of them. You can't ride into the bushes without chaps—otherwise the thorns would tear your legs to pieces. As you saw, farther on, where the big ranches start, the plains are clearer. But wherever you go, you're never too far from these thickets if you want to run and hide. And these thickets stretch down to the Rio Grande, in case you need to cross over into Mexico."

"You're saying to me we're not going to flush Crazy Joe Fields out of there?" Doc asked.

"There's no way of getting him out. Or hundreds of others like him."

"We only want Joe," Doc said.

"We're going to have to make him come after us."

"You got any ideas?"

Raider smiled. "I thought *you* might be good as bait."

"I had a feeling you had something in store for me."

"You know how Crazy Joe seems to know everything that happens in town?" Raider said. "I think informants listen around town and feed him information on likely targets to rob."

"I'm going to be the target."

"That's right," Raider said. "I've already put out word on you. I've been talking about how you've been hired by some of the big landowners to move gold and silver coins upriver for them."

Doc smiled. "That doesn't sound a very likely story. Why would they do that?"

"Who knows? Joe is crazy anyway, so he won't know the difference. Even if he has his doubts about the story, you'll be such easy prey for him—a lone man on a wagon pulled by a lone mule—it will be worth his while to bushwhack you to see what you might have.''

"Where will you be while I'm being bushwhacked?" Doc inquired politely.

"In the wagon behind you."

"Glad to hear it."

"Only thing is," Raider added, "you should start right away."

"But it's going to be sundown in a couple of hours."

"That's what we want them to see—you leaving town with the wagon at sunset. They'll guess you'll be staying at a ranch and making an early start from there unobserved. That will send Joe's informant out to see him tonight."

"You want me to sleep under my wagon out in the thickets?" Doc asked.

"You've done it many times before."

"Not when I've been within reach of a decent bed."

Raider shook his head. "Since you been chasing that blonde, bed is all you think about anymore."

Doc looked stung. "You got no use for a bed with that governess."

Doc moved out at dawn, north along the left bank of the Pecos. He wondered why Raider could have imagined anyone would want to send their gold and silver out into this wilderness in a mule-drawn wagon. When Raider arrived from town, he asked him.

"I don't know," Raider said. "I've never had enough gold or silver of my own to get to worrying about it."

Raider hid his horse in a shady thicket in which mesquite grass was growing and climbed aboard the wagon. Doc called to Judith, who moved forward more agreeably than usual. On his right the sun had now cleared the horizon. Jackrabbits scampered through the scrub, and all sorts of small animals and insects made themselves busy before the heat of mid-morning struck. Doc was in no hurry, but even at this slow pace the wagon jolted and shook over the rough trail. Hundreds of Doc's litle medicine bottles rattled in their crates at every bump.

"We got horsemen coming up behind us," Raider called in warning from his hiding place on the wagon.

"Don't shoot them," Doc warned. "They could be honest travelers."

Doc didn't turn his head until they were alongside the wagon, passing him singly on the narrow trail. As they passed, each of the four eyed the contents of the wagon. This was not unusual—folks were always curious about the strange goods Doc carried around with him. They seemed friendly enough and went ahead on their way.

"I seen all four of them in the saloons in town," Raider called in a low voice from his hiding place. "I think I told one of them about you carrying all that gold."

He had hardly finished saying this when the wagon rounded a curve in the trail and the four horsemen stood abreast across it, facing Doc. Doc pulled on Judith's reins and the wagon lurched to a halt a hundred yards from the mounted men. They purposefully and unhurriedly pulled their rifles from their saddle scabbards.

"Git off that wagon," one of them shouted, bringing his rifle to his shoulder.

"Duck!" Raider yelled at Doc.

As Doc threw himself flat on the driver's bench, the revolving cluster of barrels of Raider's Gatling gun spat lead over his prone body, over the startled mule's head, in a deadly swath across the chests of the four mounted men.

They were cut clean from their horses. All four animals bolted, unhurt.

"Damn," was all Doc said as he fetched his derby from the floor of the wagon and dusted it off with his cuff.

Raider put down the Gatling, jumped off the wagon, and patted Judith on the neck.

"Hardly moved a muscle, did you, old girl," Raider said playfully. "I thought I might have nicked a piece out of your big mule ears. I had to shoot between them."

He and Doc walked forward to examine the bodies of the four men scattered over the trail.

"I guess we should pull them off the trail a little ways and let the buzzards have them," Raider said. When Doc looked distasteful, he added, "Unless of course you want to take them back to town on your wagon and explain them to the sheriff."

Doc sighed, reached under the armpits of one corpse, and hauled the man into the scrub with his spurred heels dragging two long lines in the dirt. They pulled all four bodies far enough from the trail so they couldn't be seen by a man on horseback. Then they returned to the wagon. Which was gone.

They ran back along the trail and saw it a quarter mile away. A man was driving the wagon, with his horse tied to the back. Neither had a rifle with him, and at this distance if they could hit anything with their revolvers, it would be more likely Judith than the thief.

"Damn fool mule," Raider muttered.

Doc glanced at him annoyed, stood, and bellowed at the top of his lungs, "Judith! Judith!"

The mule came to such a sudden stop that the man was almost pitched headfirst from the wagon.

Raider and Doc laughed and began to run forward. The

wagon driver spent some moments trying to beat the mule forward, but she wouldn't budge. Then, rifle in hand, he climbed back into the wagon and searched among Doc's cures and remedies. As they neared, he took shots with his rifle at them and slowed their progress by making them dodge from scrub to scrub along the sides of the trail. Before they got within accurate pistol range, the man abandoned his search and freed his horse. He mounted, waved his rifle at them, and cantered off along the trail.

"Any idea who that might have been?" Doc asked wearily, surveying his scattered medicines on the wagon.

Raider laughed. "Joe Fields is crazy all right, like a fox."

"I feel so foolish," she said. "It turns out I am the only one, apart from his children, who did not know."

Raider looked across the table at the earnest face of Sarah Cooper, governess to the children of Noah Blake. He asked her, "You didn't tell his wife, did you?"

"I wouldn't do that. But if I had, it wouldn't have mattered. She knew everything. Apparently there's been a whole series of ladies before this blond one, according to what I've been told. I had looked up to Mr. Blake so much as the ideal husband and father that it came as quite a shock to find out he . . . he has a woman on the side. Everyone out at the ranch has heard that a traveling physician has taken this blonde away from the boss. They think it very funny, especially because Mr. Blake is in very bad humor these days and complains about everything. I wonder what they'd say if they knew I'd been introduced to this doctor. He is a fascinating character, isn't he?"

"Oh, he certainly is," Raider agreed without much enthusiasm. "What I don't understand is that whole setup at the Tumbling K Ranch. Doc said it sounds more like a proper Bostonian household than the homestead of a Texas rancher.''

"Mr. Blake is from Philadelphia, like me," Sarah said. "In fact, we're distant cousins, though I'm from the poorer branch of the family."

She rambled on about Philadelphia, Noah Blake's success as a cattle baron, how he had returned east for a wife, who insisted that their children be prepared by a governess for school back east when the time came. Sarah herself had come to Texas following the death of her husband after only two years of marriage. She admitted to being naive, but she was not such an angel as she might appear to be in Raider's view. She batted her eyelashes at him when she said that, which made him feel he might be getting somewhere with her.

"Men out here in Texas are so *coarse*," she was saying to him. "Doc Weatherbee is different. He's a proper gentleman."

This annoyed Raider. He was the one who was behaving like a proper gentleman—not Doc, who was doing as he pleased. Yet Doc got the credit. Raider said nothing. When he was not with Sarah, Raider often wondered what the hell he was doing with this woman who hardly let him kiss her lightly on the cheek, and that only after several meetings. Yet when he was with her, all such thoughts were far from his mind. Her face had a sweet look—that was all he could call it. Something sweet and trusting in it melted his hard old heart and tamed him temporarily.

Raider's attention was caught by a tall man who strode into the saloon, leaving the batwing doors swinging after him. The stranger was dressed in black, had a long thin face and a long thin nose, and his watery blue eyes had a deadened gaze. Raider was on the lookout for associates of Joe Fields in town, and this man was a good candidate for that, in his opinion. Raider saw that others knew who he was and deferentially made way for him at the bar.

An acquaintance of Raider's joined them at their table. "That's Mournful John McClintock," he said, referring to the man in black, "the famous bounty hunter. I bet he's heard of the five thousand reward on Crazy Joe's head and has come to collect it. They say he's like a weasel—once he's got his teeth sunk in someone, he never lets go. Never brings a man in alive, neither. You might say he enjoys his work."

"I've heard about him," Sarah said, to Raider's surprise. "Mr. Blake was talking about him the other day. Isn't he the one who uses a knife tip to carve a teardrop in each of his bullets?"

"That's him," Raider's acquaintance confirmed. "It's like his signature, I suppose."

Doc Weatherbee sat in a tub of warm soapy water, smoking an Old Virginia cheroot and sipping on a glass of Mexican red mission wine. Holding his wineglass in his left hand and the cheroot between his teeth, he brushed Adele's blond curls from her eyes with his right hand and allowed his fingers to wander over her bare shoulder and down her back as she knelt naked beside the tub, her arms up to the elbows in the water. Her sensitive small hands delicately fondled his balls and stroked his hard prick.

His right hand glided down over her shapely smooth back, following her firm flesh as it narrowed into her waist and then swelled out into her hip. His palm cupped one soft globe of her ass and gently squeezed it.

Like a maddened old bull alligator, Doc emerged suddenly from the water in a rush, sloshing suds in all directions. He seized the blonde's lithe body as she screamed and struggled. Her golden skin was lubricated against his by the soapy water, and they both enjoyed the tantalizing friction of their skins. She got to her feet, facing him, and he felt his cock slip in between her thighs, felt her nestle his manhood against her crotch, and the violent surge in his member almost lifted her off the floor.

They never reached the bed, settling for a buffalo skin spread on the floor.

"Fuck me, please!" she gasped, maneuvering her belly beneath his and, with a placid sigh, raising her knees and opening her legs.

Doc's prong accepted her offer eagerly. Its bulbous head forced its way between the outer lips of her hungry sex, and was greeted by the warm vacuum of her moist trembling tissues. He drove his manhood deep within her trembling, surrendering body—feeling the majesty and justice of his might in her whimpered acquiescence to his forceful drives.

As he drove himself deep within her, she answered his thrusts with the wild rhythm of her hips. She bucked wildly beneath him, threshed frenziedly, bit savagely into his shoulder. Then he felt her body flex tightly, and she pulled him close to her, preventing him from moving. Rapid shudders racked her body, and she clung to him as wave after wave of orgasmic spasms rippled through her flesh.

When she was done, she urged him to new effort by clasping his buttocks in her hands and pulling his member deep within her. Doc pumped and hammered for all he was worth, until all his efforts burst into a stream of hot gism which he shot into her with a hot flame of pleasure.

• • •

Judith's supply of oats and water was generous. Doc had left Adele asleep in his hotel room and stopped by the Horseshoe Saloon on his way to the stables. He sat with Raider and Sarah Cooper for a drink, and they had pointed out Mournful John McClintock to him. They had walked with him to the livery stables, where Raider was now seeing Sarah off in her horse and buggy. She had an hour's ride to the Tumbling K, Blake's ranch, but lots of daylight to do it in. Doc had taken the opportunity to visit his beloved Judith.

While Doc was in the stall tending to the mule, the stableman had a visitor with seemingly urgent news. The stableman quieted down the newcomer's eager voice, no doubt gesturing back to where Doc was. They didn't want to be overheard. Doc guessed from the tone of the stableman's voice that he already knew what the newcomer's news was. Doc suspected that the man's news was that Mournful John McClintock was in town and looking for Crazy Joe Fields, but that the stableman already knew because he had stabled McClintock's horse.

Fields would be shot on sight by many of the townspeople who hated his guts for having harmed or robbed them or someone close to them. Yet there were others—like the hotel clerk—who didn't hide their sympathies for the outlaw. The stableman had never said anything to Doc about Crazy Joe. Mournful John's arrival had set Doc to thinking that Joe's friends in town would want him to know about this as soon as possible. It would be hopeless to try to follow someone on horseback out of the town either by day or night—concealment was impossible. A horseman riding into or out of town in the dark would be noticed too. Except around the livery stables. They were on the edge of town, a couple of hundred yards from the nearest building, separated by a large corral.

Doc waited for Raider to appear. Doc was spending his afternoons in the hotel room with Adele, after which he would come down for dinner and then play cards and drink whiskey in one of the saloons. He was up the next day before dawn and out scouting the ranches and country about the town till the midday heat drove him back to his hotel room and Adele. The days went by.

Doc knew Raider was getting nowhere with Sarah Cooper, that he was too hot for her to bother with other women, couldn't win a dime on three aces, didn't sleep well at night because of snoring in the next room. . . . Plus the fact that Crazy Joe had outwitted them and spoiled Raider's plan. Perhaps if they got Joe this time, it would lift the jinx on Raider and end his run of bad luck.

When Raider showed, they left the stables and Doc explained his plan to him. Raider didn't waste time criticizing Doc's strategy—that wasn't his style. Raider liked to try a thing. If it worked, it worked. He didn't brood or worry.

They ate separately in the dining room of the Hotel Williamville and at dark went to two different saloons, those nearest the livery stables. When it was fully night, each made his way through back lots behind the buildings till they came to the rails of the corral, the meeting place agreed upon.

Doc could barely see the weathered pine rails of the corral by starlight. They waited there to allow their eyes to grow accustomed to the dark, then ducked between the rails and crossed the corral to the rear of the stables. It had been fully dark for less than half an hour, so they figured they would have a longish wait before Crazy Joe showed, if he ever did. They saw a glow of lamplight from a rear stable window.

Raider and Doc eased their way up to the window and peered in. Crazy Joe sat at a rough table, eating meat and beans with a spoon from a tin plate. They watched him slug from a bottle of beer, an expensive drink in this part of Texas.

"I bet he sleeps here too," Raider whispered.

"Maybe he sends into town for a girl to keep him company," Doc said drily.

"And we've been dragging our asses all over them hot dusty plains, looking for him."

They drew their revolvers and stood for a moment on each side of the door. Then Raider kicked it inward and dashed inside. He leveled his gun barrel at Joe's forehead as the outlaw was shoveling a spoonful of kidney beans into his mouth. Joe's mouth closed around the spoon and wiped it clean. He began to chew the food loudly, looking up at Raider with his strange bright eyes. Raider said nothing but reached around and took Joe's revolver from its holster. Doc too was covering the outlaw now, having checked the inside of the stable. No one else was there. Which might not be the case for long.

"Get up," Raider said to Joe.

"I want to finish my food first," Joe said calmly.

"I'll buy you a good dinner from the Hotel Williamville and have it sent to your cell," Raider offered.

Joe continued eating. "Why don't you boys shoot me here and have done with it? I ain't worth an extra penny to you alive, so why're you taking the risk?"

"We're Pinkertons," Doc said.

Joe went on chewing and looked them over. "You

meant what you said about that first-class dinner you was
going to send me in the town jail?''

Raider nodded.

Joe Fields got to his feet and walked toward the door.
Doc stopped him and they searched him. They took a
derringer from his left boot.

"So Crazy Joe was eating dinner here in town every
night and I knew nothing about it," Sheriff Jackson Dean
drawled unconcernedly. "You boys were mighty sharp to
bag him there. How come you never said nothing to me
about being Pinkertons while you was here in town?''

"We figured you have enough on your hands as it is,
Sheriff, without us bothering you with our problems,''
Doc said smoothly.

The sheriff looked none too pleased. "My one concern
here is you boys making me look foolish.''

"I don't think too much will be made of Joe Fields's
movements or whereabouts at the trial," Doc said. "There's
lots of major things—such as murders—for them to be
distracted with in Joe's case.''

The sheriff brightened. "That's for sure. You fellas got
to understand I have to take care of the whole county, and
it's not my fault if this town is too stingy to pay a
marshal . . .''

When the sheriff had stepped away for a moment, Doc
said to Raider, "I don't trust him to hold Joe prisoner.
We're going to have to take it in turns to stand guard
here.''

By way of an answer, Raider indicated the window.
Almost twenty men, some of them swigging from bottles,
had gathered in the dark street outside the sheriff's office.
The glow of the window illuminated their angry faces.

The sheriff came in the door from the street. "Seems like we could have trouble outside. I'm trusting that no more than what we have already are going to show. If they do, we got a lynch mob on our hands." He unlocked a gun rack against one wall and handed Raider and Doc each a double-barreled shotgun. "It might cool them off if they see us getting ready for them."

"I think you should move them away from here right now, Sheriff," Doc said. "You're going to get a lot of jokers from the saloons in a short while who'll just stop by for a little entertainment if they see these men gathered here."

"This is my town," Jackson Dean said. "We do it like I say. If we go out now, we'll just be making trouble."

"That's not the way I see it," Raider put in.

"Too bad, fella," Dean muttered and peered through the window at the men outside. "You should know there ain't a judge due in this town for another month. Nearest place I know where you could find one would be San Carlos, two days' ride upriver from here."

"We'll leave with Fields tomorrow," Doc said.

"Can't you get some deputies to help you here?" Raider asked.

"Hell, I can see two men out there who I often deputize." The sheriff shook his head. "There's too many folks in this town who'd like to see quick justice done to Joe Fields. Us three are on our own."

"Glad to see you're on our side," Raider commented.

"Way I see it, I ain't working with the Pinkertons," Dean replied. "I'm just preventing a man in my custody from being lynched. Matter of personal pride. That's all."

The crowd outside the sheriff's office was getting bigger as men drifted by to join it in twos and threes. As their numbers grew, so did their confidence. They now looked back boldly at the three men inside facing them with shotguns. A bulky man in a new straw hat pushed his way to the front of the mob.

"Crazy Joe Fields ain't leaving Williamville without paying for his crimes against us all!" the man shouted.

This was greeted by a cheer, and the crowd began to stir ominously in the dark street.

"We know the sheriff of this town," the man went on in a loud voice. "Jackson Dean is doing the best job he knows how. But by now he's got to see that the people of Williamville want justice done. And they want it done in Williamville!"

More cheers.

"This fella sounds like he's running for mayor," Raider said.

Doc shouted at the crowd through the open window. "Joe Fields is being brought to justice. We'll stand him in front of a judge in San Carlos in a couple of days. That judge says what will happen, not any of you. So you can all go away now. Quit wasting your time."

"If we want Joe Fields, we can come in and get him," the heavy man in the straw hat yelled back. "The sheriff's not going to stop us."

"You'll have to take Joe Fields over the bodies of two dead Pinkertons," Doc rasped.

Raider pointed the double barrels of his shotgun directly at the heavy man. "I'm going to bring a lot of you with me when I go."

The sheriff stayed quiet. So did the crowd, sensing that these Pinkertons meant what they said. But the man in the straw hat was not going to give in. He ranted on to the mob and tried to stir them up. Doc and Raider could get the sheriff to do nothing, and they reckoned they themselves had better hold off till the real trouble started.

Joe Fields sat quietly in his cell, not making a sound.

"They can't stop us!" the heavy man was yelling. "You! You there! You're Mournful John McClintock. What have you got to say? Are you with us?"

A pool of light illuminated McClintock's sour visage and black-clad body. He strutted up to the door of the sheriff's office and, before entering, turned to the mob.

"In my book," he said, "a court-ordered hanging's just as good as any street lynching. Let the judge string him up."

"To hell with you, McClintock!" the heavy man bellowed in a burst of rage. "You do your bounty hunting somewhere else from now on. The citizens of Williamville don't want you in their town."

Silence descended as the crowd waited to see how McClintock would react to the heavy man's bluster. The bounty hunter was opening the office door and stepping inside, ignoring the taunt, when the heavy man called after him again.

"You heard what I said, McClintock!" he shouted, now reckless because he sensed a personal victory over this famous gunman. "Join us or get out of town! That's the choice I'm offering—"

His words were drowned out in a gunshot, and his straw hat was lifted clean off his head by a bullet from Mournful John McClintock's revolver, revealing his bald dome. His mouth hung open in fright, but no sounds came from it. The crowd laughed and began to drift away.

CHAPTER FOUR

Doc Weatherbee arrived at the sheriff's office shortly after dawn the next day with steak and eggs and a quart of coffee for Raider and Crazy Joe. Doc had taken the first four-hour watch, and Raider the second. The sheriff had been pleased to go home to bed.

"How you boys aiming to get me out of town in one piece?" Joe asked.

"That lynch mob from last night will be sleeping off their hangovers," Doc said. "Anyone who gets ideas has to face Raider and me. We just got to watch no one shoots you in the back with a long shot from a rifle."

"Yeah, we got to think of that," Joe said, pouring himself another cup of coffee.

Joe was so calm and cooperative, it was as if they were all arranging to do something together of their own free will. Doc guessed his attitude would change once they were safely out of Williamville. From Joe's viewpoint, the two men who were taking him to be hanged in San Carlos were the same two who were saving him from the rope in Williamville. In his situation he had to play for time and hope it brought some twist of fortune.

They walked from the sheriff's office to the livery stables on the edge of town without incident. Raider walked along the street immediately behind Crazy Joe, and his height and broad shoulders blocked out the view for any backshooter in the buildings they passed. Doc's eyes swept the storefronts and windows before them.

"I'll be back for my mule and wagon," Doc told the stableman. "Don't get any ideas that just because we pulled in your friend Joe Fields, you're going to take it out on my mule. You're damn lucky you're not being charged with aiding and abetting Fields—which makes you an accessory to murder." Doc let this sink in. "If that mule's flanks aren't sleek and glossy and if her belly ain't full of your best oats, she's going to tell me. Got that?"

"That mule tells him everything," Raider added in a serious tone.

The stableman looked impressed.

"This ain't no friend of mine who will be looking to revenge me," Joe said, looking at the stableman in disgust. "Everything he ever gave me I had to pay for in gold at three times its cost. He's going to miss Joe Fields for his easy money."

They rode out of town north along the narrow, deep, muddy river in its steep banks. Groves of willows and cottonwoods grew next to the water but thinned out to thorny scrub within a few paces. Doc and Raider knew that the thickets would thin out gradually into a level, treeless plain, which they would have all the way to San Carlos. Once they reached the plain, they could keep out of rifle range from the river bank and see anyone approach long before they came within striking distance. However, until they gained the plain, they would have to rely on their quiet exit and vigilance for safety. Out here in the thorny scrub, a whole regiment could lay hiding in wait for them and be invisible.

Raider rode in front, his Model 94 Winchester lever-action .30-.30 caliber carbine resting crossways before him on the saddle, with a bullet in its firing chamber. The carbine's short barrel made it an ideal weapon for use on horseback, where a full-length rifle barrel was much more awkward to handle in spite of its greater accuracy. Crazy Joe came next. His wrists were loosely bound to his saddle pommel. Doc Weatherbee brought up the rear. His Winchester .44-.40 rifle hung in the crook of his right arm, and his eyes never ceased scanning the brush to each side of them for a movement or a glint of metal.

Doc saw nothing. He only heard the shot. And saw Raider pitch forward in the saddle and slide headfirst in a helpless bundle onto the ground.

Doc looked wildly about him, then felt a terrible pain in his chest and shoulder and saw the gray earth swoop up to hit him. He knew he had been shot. He lay absolutely still, ignoring the pain, and tried to see what was happening without moving his head.

Raider lay where he fell. Doc could not tell if he was still breathing. Crazy Joe was making good his escape, spurring his horse off the trail, away from the river. He didn't get far before a horseman cantered after him through the thickets, caught his horse's rein, and led it back to the trail. The rider sat tall in the saddle and was dressed in black. It was Mournful John McClintock.

So that was why the bounty hunter had helped them previous night against the lynch mob. He wanted Joe

Fields's neck spared all right—so he could collect the bounty on his head. In spite of the pain—or perhaps because of it—Doc was thinking crystal clear. He doubted if McClintock had scratched teardrops on the bullets he had used on Raider and him. There would be times when Mournful John would not wish to leave his signature. He would claim that Crazy Joe or someone else had shot the two Pinkertons and that he had come across Joe only after their deaths. Which made one thing very plain to Doc— neither he nor Raider nor Crazy Joe was meant to live to tell any tales about what had really happened.

Doc shut his eyes and stayed motionless as Mournful John rode back toward him along the trail. He heard the hooves pause a moment as the rider gave him and Raider a quick look over where they lay, and then the hooves stamped the ground as McClintock's horse turned in its tracks and moved away again, followed by Crazy Joe's horse in tow. Doc's horse seemed to have bolted. Raider's, too.

He clenched his teeth against the pain in his chest and opened his eyes to a slit. Mournful John had stopped his horse again, about thirty yards away. Crazy Joe sat in the saddle of the horse behind him, his wrists still bound to the saddle pommel. McClintock replaced his rifle in its scabbard. He said something to Crazy Joe, but Doc could not hear the words. Then the bounty hunter calmly drew his revolver and shot Crazy Joe. Joe's horse shied and pulled on the rope tied to McClintock's saddle. The bounty hunter fired again, and Joe slumped, half on and half off his horse.

McClintock dismounted and untied Joe's bonds from the pommel but not from his wrists. He pulled Joe across the horse's back so that his arms hung down one side and his legs down the other. McClintock drew the loose ends of the rawhide bonds beneath the horse's belly and tied them to Joe's ankles, thus securing his body on the horse. He then remounted and rode away with the horse in tow. He never looked back.

Doc waited till he was quite sure McClintock had gone. He moved his head and looked about. He and Raider were alone. Raider lay absolutely still where he had fallen, and Doc could see a spreading bloodstain on his shirt. Doc decided it was safe now to go to his aid and went to raise himself on his elbows.

A searing agony leveled him, and he almost lost consciousness. After a while—he could not tell how long— the nausea and dizziness subsided and Doc tried to raise himself up on his elbows again. Once more he was leveled by red-hot pain. When his head cleared, he realized he had further weakened himself by his two efforts to rise. Slowly it dawned on him that he was trapped out here without being able to move.

"Raider!" he called as loudly as he could, which was little better than a throaty rasp. "Raider . . ."

There was no reply. No movement that he could see in Raider's body.

Doc twisted his head about in a vain search for something to aid him. There was only the parched gray soil and whatever the thorny scrub concealed. Above him the sky was a merciless blue. It was quite early in the morning, so the sun's heat was still bearable.

Far off three black specks floated against the blue. Buzzards searching for carrion . . .

The Pecos Large Holdings Association was holding a breakfast meeting at the Tumbling K Ranch. Noah Blake sat at the head of the long table and beamed at his fellow big landowners over the bacon, sausages, and eggs set on large silver platters up and down the table. They waited to discuss their business until they had finished eating. After Blake had sent a servant around the table with a bottle of French brandy to spike their coffee, he got down to brass tacks.

The owner of the Tumbling K had been carefully studying his companions while they ate. Including himself, all fourteen of the biggest landowners in the area were present. Six of them, again including himself, were men of old established families back east or in the South who had come to Texas to build new family empires and who had the backing of banks and wide business connections. They attempted to live in the style of the country gentlemen they had known before coming to Texas. The other eight cattle barons were of a rougher breed. Most had obtained their lands by hiring men to make adjoining homesteading claims, each for the maximum acreage permitted, and then putting all the pieces together in one large whole. Blake knew the backgrounds of some of these men: They were tough, they did not scare easily, and they were greedy. Each group— the inheritors of wealth and the self-made men—did not think much of the other, yet all knew how to unite when their common interests were at stake.

Blake said, "Hope you enjoyed breakfast, gentlemen, particularly the eggs—because if we don't do something soon about cattle rustlers, we're all going to end up as chicken farmers."

He knew that was all he needed to say to get the fierier ranchers going. Some of the men spoke quietly and tersely; others ranted and exaggerated; none were indifferent. He listened at the head of the table as the talk and tempers heated up. He rang the service bell now and then for more coffee and brandy. Noah Blake, like every man at the table, had heard all this talk and all these threats before. But this time he intended it to be different. This time they would take action. If he had to keep them around the table for lunch or even dinner as well as breakfast, Blake was determined that this meeting would not break up—as had so many others—without a definite plan of action agreed upon and set in motion.

"If I may attempt a summing up, gentlemen," Blake contributed, "the big problem is that bands of rustlers often number between twelve and fifteen men, are highly skilled at handling cattle, and are well armed and shoot to kill."

There was a murmur of assent around the table.

Blake went on, "Cowhands, even when honest and hardworking, can't respond against such superior force. It seems to matter very little whether the cattle are driven south across the border or northeast to a railhead. In either event they are impossible to trace if given more than a half a day's start. I think it's fair to say that so far things have been going the rustlers' way, and that so long as this remains the case, the more rustlers and rustling we're going to see in the future." He looked up and down the table at every face. "Unless we do something about it." His fist crashed on the table. "Now!"

That brought him a round of applause.

"What I propose," Noah Blake continued, "is that we put a bounty of three hundred dollars on the head of every rustler killed on our lands. This will attract gunfighters and bounty hunters who will clear these vermin for us. If each of us here today agrees to pay on presentation of the dead rustler, we will have a successful deterrent finally in place."

The vote of approval was unanimous.

"I just got one thing to say in disagreement," one rancher spoke up. "I don't think it's only *bandidos* and local organized rustlers who are stealing my cattle. I'm damn sure a lot of them are being taken by local small ranchers."

Blake responded, "I'll pay a bounty to the killer of any small rancher who tries to steal cattle on my land."

Everyone was happy with that.

The Comanche rode his big bay stallion slowly and silently among the thickets, moving cautiously and blending with his background. He had waited all morning and they had not come. They would not come today. At dawn tomorrow he would wait again.

His horse needed water. He rode out of the cover of the thorny scrub and crossed the trail on his way to the river bank. Something caught his eye. A body. Farther down the trail. Two white men lay shot on the ground. A nice carbine lay near one—he could use that.

Doc moaned with relief when the man standing over him blocked out the rays of the sun with his body. Doc's lips and tongue were swollen with thirst—he could no longer close his mouth, and fine dust was caked inside, partway down his throat. The man stood above him, without bending, and poured water from a leather pouch into Doc's mouth so that it flooded over, ran down his chin and splashed in his eyes. He felt the water hit the interior of his stomach. His insides contracted from the shock of the cool water and he half regurgitated the liquid. The man above him laughed and stopped pouring.

"Never thought you'd see that much water again, did you?" he asked.

"Is my friend alive?" Doc croaked.

"Dunno. I'll go see." The man walked over to Raider's prone form. "He's still breathing, but it looks like he's been hit bad. He won't last much longer if he don't get in out of this sun."

Doc's vision cleared, and he was surprised to see the man was an Indian.

"Pull us both into the shade of those prickly pears, if you will," Doc asked.

"If you gotta die, you'll go quicker left out in the sun," the Indian pointed out. "You'll die slower in the shade. Maybe the coyotes will tear you to pieces tonight while you're still alive."

"I'll take my chances on that," Doc told him.

The Indian dragged both of them into the shade of the prickly pears. He was stocky, broad-shouldered, and extremely strong. He wore no tribal decorations of any kind and dressed in denims almost bleached white by exposure to the sun. His long black hair was thick and glossy and hung about his face down to his shoulders, not restrained by a headband.

"You want me to give your friend water?" he inquired.

Doc nodded.

The Indian propped Raider up and got him to swallow water by massaging his throat. This was obviously not the first time he had rescued a man on the sunbaked plains. It occurred to Doc that "rescue" might be too strong a word. The Indian had made it plain that he thought they should remain in the sun in order to die more quickly. Those did not sound like the words of a man who intended to rescue them by bringing them back to town.

"You come from Williamville or you go there?" the Indian asked.

"We left first thing this morning."

"You ever hear of a man named Fields? They call him Crazy Joe."

"Sure." Doc was on his guard.

"I hear he was captured. They hang him or what?"

"No," Doc said. "Two Pinkerton agents were to take him to San Carlos to stand trial."

"Yes, I'm waiting for them," the Indian said.

"You're lying in ambush too?" Doc asked, incredulous.

"Crazy Joe is my friend. I kill those Pinkertons and set him free."

Doc tried to laugh, but he had to stop because of the pain. "You're late. We're the Pinkertons."

The Indian pondered this a moment. "Where is Joe?"

Doc realized he would need to be careful about this. "We were bushwhacked. Ever hear of Mournful John McClintock?"

"He has hunted me maybe five, six times," the Indian said scornfully. "He had to give up every time."

The fact that this Indian claimed to be a friend of Crazy Joe's should have been enough to suggest he was an outlaw too. He must be a dangerous one, Doc thought, if the price on his head was high enough to attract the likes of Mournful John into several unsuccessful attempts.

"McClintock attacked us. He took Crazy Joe."

"You lie to me," the Indian said fiercely.

Doc decided to tell the whole truth. "He shot him in cold blood just down the trail there, tied him over his saddle, and left with his horse tied behind his own."

The Indian's expression never changed. His almost black eyes pierced into Doc's for a long while. Then he said slowly, "So my friend Joe Fields is dead. Shot in cold blood by McClintock. Were Joe's hands bound?"

"Yes."

"You saw it happen?"

"Yes."

The Indian exhaled a deep sigh. "I too saw Mournful John McClintock. Farther north along the trail. I did not know it was him then—but now I know that it was. A tall white man with black clothes and a packhorse behind him. So I thought. I did not know my friend's dead body was passing close to me as I watched and let his murderer go unhindered."

Doc was surprised at the quality of this Indian's English, but he had met Indians before who had attended mission schools on reservations, and they had been better educated than many of the white men around. Doc ruefully remembered his own school days and what a strict teacher with a big stick could do to get a boy reading the Bible word perfect. The Indian went on blaming himself as Doc wondered how to persuade him to help Raider and him back to Williamville. Doc needed to think. He couldn't let his wound or physical condition interfere. Listening to the Indian, it was soon clear to Doc that he had only one chance at success.

"If I ever get out of here," Doc interrupted him, "the first thing I'll do when I get better is go after Mournful John McClintock."

The Indian stopped talking and looked carefully at him. He finally said, "*I* will kill Mournful John McClintock."

"How can you find him? Aren't you on the run from the law?"

The Indian scowled and said nothing.

"You can't go into towns," Doc said. "He might never come back this way again. Or he might pass through in ten days' time and you will miss him. Again."

Doc saw that barb sink beneath the Indian's skin.

"We're Pinkertons. We can find him anywhere. All I need do is go to the telegraph office and I'll find where he is. If you want your revenge, get us into town."

The Indian shook his head. "If you kill him, that will be no good to me. *I* must kill him with these two hands." He held them up for Doc to see. "You must get him for me."

Doc had no intention of promising to capture Mournful John in order to hand him over to an Indian outlaw. "If we capture him, he has to go to jail. Of course you could come along and help us capture him."

The Indian's eyes glinted. "I believe you speak the truth. I have your word on that?"

"We will contact you as soon as we locate Mournful John and wait for you before going after him. I promise that."

The Indian tore away part of the front of Doc's shirt. "High in the shoulder. Your friend was also hit in the right shoulder but lower down. It will go harder with him. Only one shot at each of you?"

"Yes."

"Where are your horses?"

"I don't know."

The Indian tapped his right nostril with a forefinger. "Horses have a nose for water. I will catch them by the river bank before dawn tomorrow."

Without another word, he walked off into the thorny scrub.

The Indian returned an hour later with an armful of small plants and four dead lizards. He gathered some dried gnarled branches and made a fire. Doc watched him spend a long time crushing the plants in water in a copper bowl and skinning the lizards and adding their skins to the mixture. He put the metal bowl over the fire and chanted over it for some minutes. Doc was damned if he was going to drink any of this stuff.

"What tribe are you?"

"Comanche."

"I thought all the Comanches had been driven out of Texas up into the Indian Territory," Doc said.

"A few of us came back." He smiled slyly at Doc and suddenly became informative. "I was only ten when they moved my family—not old enough to be a warrior or I would have died rather than go. My father, mother, all my family died of white-man diseases up in the Indian Territory. Not my father. No. He died of a broken heart. I was put in a boarding school for Indians. When I was old enough, I ran away and came back here. I was fourteen when I returned—old enough to be a warrior. Back then white men called me the Comanche Kid. Some still do. I have other names. The boarding school gave me a fool white man's name that I never use. No white man ever learned my real name, my Comanche name. The Spanish-speaking people call me El Caballito del Diablo. I like that."

Doc said, "I've heard of you."

The Indian looked pleased. "I am very bad and have killed lots of my enemies."

"I see."

"But Pinkertons would not chase me unless they were hired to do it."

"That's right," Doc agreed enthusiastically. "And we haven't been hired to do that."

"I will take you to town tomorrow. Close to it, because I can't go there. A Mexican family named Sanchez live in the foothills on the other side of the Pecos. They will find me for you. All this is secret."

"Absolutely," Doc assured him. "Isn't there any chance you'd get us into Williamville today rather than tomorrow?"

"First I have to fix your wounds. There is no doctor in Williamville. My medicine"—he pointed to the copper pot on the fire—"is better than you can get there."

Caballito ignored Doc from then on and went to work on Raider. He tore away the shirt from his right shoulder, exposing the entry wound of the rifle bullet. Then he pulled out a Mexican knife with a long, thin blade which he waved in the air a few times before using it to dig out the bullet low in Raider's shoulder. Despite being unconscious, Raider moaned and moved one arm as the Indian probed his wound. He extracted a twisted lead slug, tossed it away, and went to the fire. He returned hurriedly to Raider with a glowing coal to cauterize the wound. Raider stirred and moaned again as the coal seared his flesh. Caballito then made up a poultice of the leaves from the copper pot, placed it over the wound, and bound it in place with strips from the torn shirt.

Caballito turned casually to Doc and said, "You're next. I don't have any firewater to deaden your pain, so you will have to do it the Indian way. Bite down on this"—he handed Doc a doubled length of rawhide cord—"and think of something valuable to you."

Doc smiled wanly and said, "Don't get blood on my suit."

The Indian nodded seriously, bent over Doc, and waved the long, thin blade in the air.

When Doc Weatherbee woke it was still dark. He remembered he had passed out from pain while Caballito was extracting the bullet from his right shoulder. With his left hand, he felt the wad of leaves that had been placed against his wound. He was kind of grateful he had lost consciousness before it came time to press the burning coal on the wound. It hurt like hell now. Raider cursed and grunted beside him as he tried to change position.

"You all right, Raider?"

"Doc! Where the hell are we? What happened?"

Raider's mind seemed clear, and Doc told him the whole story.

"Where's Caballito now?" Raider asked.

"Maybe he's gone to catch our horses down by the river."

"I'm in no shape to ride a horse," Raider said.

The Comanche soon returned with both their horses. He hitched the horses nearby and left again without saying anything. In a few minutes, as they began to make out their surroundings in the first gray light of day, they heard a shot. Caballito returned with a jackrabbit. Doc noted that he used the same long Mexican knife to disembowel and skin the rabbit that he had used on them. After the rabbit had been grilled over the fire and they had eaten its tough, gamy meat, Caballito began to bind willow boughs he had collected by the river between the saddles of their two horses. Slowly he constructed a platform about four feet wide across the backs of the two horses, who could now only move side by side.

He stood Raider on his feet and, with remarkable strength, eased him up over the rump of a horse onto the platform. He had less trouble with Doc, who was lighter and more mobile. Finally the two lay next to each other on the platform of boughs. The pain caused by the horses' movement over the rough trail kept both of them quiet.

They were in view of Williamville when El Caballito del Diablo stopped his own horse and urged theirs on.

He called after them, "Pinkertons, remember your promise to me. And don't let those town fools remove those leaves for one more day. I prayed over them. They are more powerful than bandages."

CHAPTER FIVE

Sarah Cooper, the governess to Noah Blake's two children, came every day to see Raider at the Hotel Williamville. He and Doc now had beds in a big, well-lighted, airy room. She was amazed at how quickly their wounds healed and that only a little infection set in. Doc's blonde, Adele, visited him for a few days and then stopped coming. They heard she had taken up with Noah Blake again. After only three days Doc was able to get about on his feet slowly.

Through Sarah, they telegraphed the Chicago office of the Pinkerton Agency to explain developments and to say they would remain in the town until they recovered and that they did not need help. So far as the agency was concerned, the case was closed with the death of Crazy Joe Fields.

A week passed before Raider took his first steps unaided. He became so weak and dizzy, he would have fallen if Doc and Sarah had not rushed to support him.

"Raider, a man your size can't expect much help on his

feet,'' Sarah gasped as she struggled to get him back to bed.

Next day Raider was taking short walks about the room and in the corridor, stopping to lean against a wall every now and then, with a look of determination on a face as white as a sheet.

The day after that he paced the room restlessly and sent down to the hotel clerk for a bottle of bourbon.

Doc passed the time reading. It went unsaid between them that he had stolen Sarah's affections away from Raider. To be more accurate, as Raider explained to himself, Doc had not *stolen* her affections from him but had aroused feelings in her that she never had for Raider. Raider was still pissed off about it, but he was made more cheerful by the way Sarah reacted to Doc as he progressed. When he was totally incapacitated at first, she was warm, loving, and sexual toward him, bestowing him with bosomy hugs and lots of soft stroking and whispers. As soon as Doc managed to get to his feet, she grew more guarded and started to ration her caresses. Now that once again he was a dangerous male capable of impregnating her, she tried to keep him at a safe distance.

This was not so easy for her to do with Doc as she had done with Raider. She had revealed a tender side of herself to Doc. He knew her weaknesses. And he was determined to exploit them. If only he could find a way around her strengths. . . .

Brad Dunwell had a ranch in a valley between the huge Tumbling K and Circle Diamond spreads. It was a relatively small holding, but at least it was his own. He could ride out on his land every bit as independently as could his neighbor Noah Blake on the Tumbling K. The valley was sheltered, providing good winter grazing for cattle, and its gently sloping sides made excellent summer pastures. A sweetwater stream that flowed all year round rose near the head of the valley, so that no animals here would ever die of drought.

The water was what Noah Blake wanted—more so than the land, which would be only a minor addition to the Tumbling K. The stream flowed from Dunwell's small ranch to the lands of the other small ranchers. To a great extent, whoever controlled the source of this stream could also control the water supplies, and thus the fortunes, of those who ranched farther down its course.

Dunwell rode some part of the boundaries of his ranch every day. Like all Texas ranchers, big and small, he did a little mavericking—any unbranded young cattle that wandered onto his spread soon ended up with his brand. He always scrupulously drove back any bearing a brand consisting of a K leaning to the right or a diamond within a circle. His own brand—a D with a quarter circle beneath it, the Rocker D—was so distinct from those of his neighbors that there had never been any accusations that he had ever altered brands. But the big ranchers claimed he stole a lot of their unbranded cattle, said he drove them off their lands onto his own.

The truth was that occasionally when his own cattle strayed and he had to drive them back, some other cattle got mixed up with them. Those with brands he always culled later and returned. Those without brands he kept. What the hell. Everyone knew that all the southern Texas ranches were originally stocked by mavericking across the border into the huge Mexican ranches. There were still lots of wild cattle in the thickets. Who could say who owned an unmarked calf?

Brad Dunwell knew that Noah Blake wanted the headwaters of that stream. All the rest was just empty talk, just threats to drive him off the land his father had claimed, worked, and died on. Brad intended to do the same, and have his son follow him.

Dunwell's horse walked contentedly in grass so deep it was halfway up its legs, with brilliant wildflowers all moving their heads at one time in a breeze. Dunwell felt the well-being of a man taking his time on his own land. He climbed the slope of the ridge separating his land from the Tumbling K and then followed a draw that cut through the ridge. Strays often came this way.

He emerged from the draw on Tumbling K land without coming across any cattle. There were none anywhere near the draw that could have strayed in from his land. He waved to a lone cowhand some way off and turned his horse to ride back through the draw to his own land.

Brad Dunwell never saw the rider behind him raise his rifle to his shoulder, and he never knew what hit him in the back.

Noah Blake's son rushed into the music room, where his sister was receiving a piano lesson from Sarah Cooper.

"A dead rustler! Mr. McClintock has brought in a dead rustler!" he shouted.

The boy did not take music lessons, because his father felt it would be unmanly for him to know how to play a piano. Sarah had disagreed with her employer on this and had appealed to the boy's mother.

"I have a brother back east who turned out no good," Mrs. Blake said. "He plays the violin."

So it was settled. Noah Blake's only son would not be exposed to the perils of musical instruments.

"Please, Mrs. Cooper! Please!" his sister piped. "Let me see the dead rustler!"

Sarah had never seen a rustler herself, dead or alive, and she imagined a wild-looking, unshaven desperado. She also knew that from Noah Blake's viewpoint no sin mentioned in the Bible came even close in seriousness to rustling. No doubt he would consider viewing a dead rustler as moral edification for his children, like hanged felons were left on crossroads gallows trees as a warning to all in medieval Europe.

The body lay on the ground by a corral. The arms lay loosely at the sides, and the man's eyes and mouth were open.

"That's not a rustler!" Blake's son said. "That's Mr. Dunwell!"

A tall man clad in black with a long face and a long nose and watery blue eyes looked disdainfully down at the children.

"Father! Father!" his son called Noah Blake. "Mr. McClintock has killed Mr. Dunwell!"

"I always knew that man was stealing from me," Blake said.

He went in the house and returned shortly to make a show of paying McClintock fifteen twenty-dollar gold pieces.

McClintock thanked him, raised his black hat courteously to Sarah, and walked away to the stables. She tried to recall where she had heard the name McClintock before.

"That's the famous Mournful John McClintock we have watching our ranges," Blake said in a pleased tone, looking down on the body of his neighbor.

Mournful John! Sarah almost shouted it aloud but stiffled her words. She would let Doc know tomorrow afternoon when she rode into town.

Mrs. Blake had joined them and was weeping softly. "What of the poor man's wife and children?"

Noah put his arm around his wife's shoulders. "Don't worry, dear. I'll give them a generous price for their land."

After Brad Dunwell's burial the next morning in the graveyard outside Williamville, the small ranchers and their families returned to the Dunwell ranch by buggy and wagon. The women brought covered pots of food they had stayed up late preparing the previous night. The men bought whiskey while they were in town—and there were so many arrangements to be made and folks they had not seen in weeks, it helped ease the dumb grief all of them felt at the death of this popular man. There was a certain purposefulness in the men's movements: For once, they were not leaving all the social arrangements up to the women. Like Blake, they knew the importance of the headwaters of that stream. Dunwell was sadly missed by them all, and the fact that he never dammed the stream to divert its water contributed much to their affection for him. Word was out that Noah Blake had already offered the widow a fair price for the land.

"She told me she don't want to go," one man's wife told him. "But she don't see how she can stay neither, what with her boys being only thirteen and ten."

Her husband asked, "You think the widow'd stay if she was offered free help from the rest of us till her boy is growed?"

"I'll ask her."

"Do that."

So many were there, the meal was eaten in four sittings. After it the men and their grown sons congregated in the shade of the barn. They drank the whiskey they had bought in town, sparingly, for it was a solemn occasion and no one wanted to show disrespect for the dead by roistering.

"The widow said she'd stay, then?" one man asked.

"If she had free help for a few years."

"She'll have mine," the first man volunteered.

"And mine."

"Mine."

Everyone offered to help.

"I guess that's settled, then," Will Tucker said. "She'll be mighty pleased to hear it. I know I'm sure relieved. None of us have the money to buy that land from her, and if Blake got his hands on that water, we'd be living on a desert farther downstream in a matter of months. He'd starve us out."

"If he don't murder us first," another man said bitterly.

"I think we got to strike back," Will Tucker announced.

This caused a sudden silence. Tucker, at twenty-eight, was no longer regarded as a hothead and hell-raiser. He had quieted down after he had got married, and now he had two children and a ranch to work. Yet, of them all, he was silently regarded as the strongest, the toughest, and now and then the meanest. If it came to taking a stand, they all looked to Will Tucker to ride out in front.

"You mean we should kill Noah Blake?" one of the older men asked a little nervously.

Tucker didn't answer.

"Shoot Blake down!" one suggested excitedly. "That will show the big landowners they can't fool with us."

"It would also give them an excuse to wipe us out in a range war, perhaps with government help," another warned.

"Noah Blake is too big a chaw for us to bite into at this

time," Tucker said, gauging the reactions around him. "I say we ride out and get the one who killed Brad Dunwell. Mournful John McClintock."

Early the next morning Will Tucker and four men saddled horses at the Dunwell Ranch, checked their rifles and revolvers, then rode toward the slopes bordering the Tumbling K. They had no heroic illusions of duelling one on one with McClintock. The five of them would catch him. Outnumbered, he would have no chance against them, and they would shoot him like a coyote.

Mournful John would be riding alone. That was his style. The ranchers had seen some other gunfighters— perhaps six in all—around the big spreads. Four Mexicans had been shot on one ranch, and two other bands of rustlers had been interrupted and chased off without casualties. Which was no good to the gunfighters—they got paid only on rustlers killed, not cattle saved.

"If we let Mournful John get away with killing Brad Dunwell," Tucker said, "those gunmen will be nosing 'round your ranch house doors, looking to nail your pelt any way they can. Don't matter to them if you're standing on your own land, not if your hide is worth three hundred dollars to them."

"That kind of work sure pays better than ranching," one man said.

Tucker patted his rifle stock and grinned. "It's high-risk work those boys do. Which is what McClintock is going to find out."

Tucker knew well enough that Mournful John McClintock had survived in his trade only because he knew how to ride out the risks. Will wouldn't say that to his companions, though—they might lose their nerve. None of them had ever lived off their ranches and, apart from some hell-raising on a Saturday night, knew little of town life. Mournful John, and others like him, were town dwellers. Will had spent enough time in the towns to know that he and his friends were country boys in the eyes of these men, that their minds were accustomed to working more slowly, that they did not live by razor-sharp perception, that they were no match for professional guns. If he had told them, they wouldn't have believed him anyway. They looked on themselves as rough and ready. Truth was, they didn't even know what a trained killer amounted to: He was a hell of a different thing from a hired cowhand who has a gripe with you and wants to settle it. Will Tucker rode on, saying nothing about this—only how they were going to teach the big ranchers a lesson by gunning down McClintock like he had gunned down their friend Brad Dunwell.

They passed through the same draw Dunwell had used to ride onto Tumbling K land. Off to their right, a lone rider spotted them. He was tall, dressed in black, and in a hell of a hurry to get out of there. The ranchers broke into two groups, one heading in direct pursuit of the galloping rider and the other bearing left, hoping to cut him off on his route to the Blake ranch house.

Will Tucker joined the group going in direct pursuit. He figured McClintock was much more likely to loop back on his pursuers or pull some crafty trick on them than travel in a straight line and allow himself to be cut off. They had taken the five best Dunwell horses, which hadn't been ridden for days, so that no horse being used to work daily was going to beat them over a long haul.

Apparently, in his panic to get away, their prey had not

noticed them split into two groups, and he was now trying to outrace them in a direct line to the ranch house, perhaps hoping that if he couldn't outrun them there, he could get close enough so they wouldn't dare follow him farther. He might even be spotted and given help by others as he neared the ranch house.

He saw the two ranchers on his left flank too late—they sat on motionless horses with rifles raised as they waited for him to get close enough for a good shot.

Tucker saw a puff of smoke from one rifle and two seconds later heard the shot as the rifleman levered another shell into the chamber. Both were rapid-firing. Their target urged his horse faster. Tucker knew the riflemen had seventeen shots apiece in their Winchester magazines—they weren't marksmen, but they could hardly miss with all thirty-four shots.

The rider's horse went down and he was thrown over its head. He jumped to his feet and ran away for a few steps till he realized the futility of it. They he ran back to where his horse lay on its side, thrashing its legs. He was obviously going for the rifle in his saddle and would take cover behind the horse.

They got him as he bent to pull the rifle free of the downed horse. He stood up straight with his arms thrown out and took a few steps backward. Then one of them hit him again, this time in the middle. He doubled over and slowly fell to the ground.

Tucker heard the cheers of his companions as they rode with him. He felt in no mood for cheering, knowing that even with McClintock out of the way, there would be another killing in reply to this one, then one in reply to that. . . .

Tucker was not prepared for the sight that met his eyes.

"That's not Mournful John McClintock," he said. "He's one of Blake's ranch hands. Been around since the beginning of the year."

"Then what did he run away for?" one of the men who did the shooting asked defensively.

"Because he was stupid," Tucker said. "It wasn't your fault. I'd have shot him too if I'd had the chance."

They covered the dead man's face with his hat so the buzzards wouldn't tear his eyeballs out. Then they rode away.

"The description fits," Doc Weatherbee admitted.

"I'm telling you it was him," Sarah Cooper insisted. "When only his last name was mentioned at first, it didn't strike me right away. But then someone said Mournful John McClintock. And you agree he looks like what I described to you. It's him!"

"I believe you," Doc said in an abstracted way. "I just wanted to be quite sure before I let myself start to feel mad."

"What are you going to do?" Sarah asked, now a little unsure of the wisdom of having told Doc the whereabouts of his assailant. She had been bursting to tell him the news, without ever reflecting on the consequences of it. She should have known what Doc's reaction would be, she thought bitterly. Say a few calming words to her and get a preoccupied look on his face. She could see that he was already plotting some bloody revenge. Men were such fools! Her information, the news she had so eagerly brought him, might end up being the cause of his death. Doc was still convalescent, and here he had already gone back to his old ways. When they left the room to have a meal, she noticed sadly that for the first time since he had been up out of bed he slipped a revolver beneath his coat.

Doc returned to his usual charming self over the meal, but she knew he was conning her. The wheels of his mind were still turning over the information she had brought him. However, it so happened that on this particular evening Sarah felt in the mood to be conned.

"Would you care to take a walk about town?" Doc asked when they had finished their meal.

"I don't think so," she said. "How about a drink in your room?"

"That's a good idea," he said enthusiastically.

She was amused at the way he tried to hide his surprise. Indeed she had shocked herself a little when she made the suggestion to him.

In his room—recovered, Doc and Raider once again had taken separate rooms—they shared some small talk over a glass of bourbon. Checking now and then to see the expression on his face, she began to disrobe in a slow and dignified way. Doc ran his eyes over the beautiful emerging body. She lay on his bed and writhed in sensuous delight in his admiring gaze. She enticed him to her with the slow, teasing rhythm of her fluid hips.

He knelt between her spread-apart thighs, leaned forward, and pressed the swollen head of his cock into the warm dampness of her pussy.

His prick pumped her in a wild rhythm, and he could hear the sound of his balls slapping against her as he drove deep on each and every thrust.

She squealed through clenched teeth and climaxed in successive convulsions until her body lay soothed and receiving beneath his.

He increased the speed and power of his thrusts, grunting and moaning as his passion grew. At last he exploded in a streaming storm inside her, and felt her body go into a fresh orgasm along with his. Their spasms went on for an incredibly long time.

CHAPTER SIX

Late that night Will Tucker approached Doc Weatherbee and Raider in the Horseshoe Saloon. They were sitting at a table, taking it easy, which was such unusual behavior for both of them that they felt ill at ease. Thus they welcomed the intrusion of this man whose sun-bronzed face and calloused hands indicated he earned a living on the land. He had more assurance in town than most, so they assumed he was no plain cowhand, though there was nothing about him to suggest he was a landowning rancher.

"You the Pinkertons that got shot?" he asked gruffly.

Doc indicated an empty chair.

"You boys all right and on your feet again?" Tucker asked.

Doc gestured vaguely. "Tolerably. As you see, we can limp into a saloon and manage to hold down a drink."

"What I have in mind would need a lot more than that," Tucker said.

"Try us." Doc poured him a whiskey from their bottle.

Will Tucker told them everything, including the killing of the innocent ranch hand by mistake. He finished his account by remarking, "You don't seem surprised to hear Mournful John McClintock is back. I heard a story he was the one who shot you two."

"We got the news already," Doc said.

"I thought you'd want to ride out to revenge yourselves," Tucker said.

"We're Pinkerton agents," Doc replied. "We can't always do what we'd like to. Now that Joe Fields is dead, the only cause we have to be in this part of Texas is that we've not yet recovered from our wounds. Of course it would be different if your organization hired us—"

"We don't even have a proper organization," Tucker objected.

"Well, get yourself one," Doc suggested. "Something on the lines of Noah Blake's Pecos Large Holdings Association."

"How about Pecos Small Ranchers League?" Tucker offered.

Doc looked across at Raider with great seriousness. "I'll let you be the judge."

Raider grinned. "Sounds great to me."

Maintaining his dignity, Doc informed Tucker, "Sir, as representative of the Pecos Small Ranchers League, you must telegraph a Mr. Wagner at the Chicago office of the Pinkerton National Detective Agency. When we receive a telegram from him, we'll be on our way."

"Good," Tucker said. "We've made such a mess of things with that mistaken killing—which we deny, needless to say—none of us know rightly what we should do next. We're professional cattlemen. They're professional killers."

"Employed by cattlemen," Doc added. "I have a few suggestions. I think the Dunwell family should be evacuated to safety. With their agreement, we'll use their ranch house as our base. You should say in your telegram to Chicago that you want us to guard the ranch in the family's absence—if you make this sound like a range war between small and large ranchers, the agency will say no. Ask for a big reduction in fees because we are incapacitated and are more or less only caretakers on the ranch. Chicago will be pleased not to have to pay our hotel bills any longer in Williamville and to have us far from trouble on an empty ranch. They'll go along with that."

Tucker looked pleased and shook hands with them both. "I'll go to the telegraph office right away. I'm stopping with a cousin a little ways outside town. When can I expect to see you boys?"

"We have an errand to run tomorrow morning," Doc said. "If that telegram gets in by noon, we'll be there by nightfall, if my colleague here agrees."

Raider nodded. "Fine with me."

Williamville started early in the day. A half hour after dawn wagons were being loaded outside the stores, men and women were going about their business on foot or by horse, and smells of strong coffee brewing wafted on the air.

"You going to be able for this ride?" Doc asked Raider as they headed for the livery stables.

"Hell, I was just going along in case you fell off and couldn't make it."

This would be the first time outside the town for either of them since being shot. They headed west out of Williamville on their hired horses. The first test they would face was crossing the Pecos. The horses had to be forced into the muddy, swirling current. The big strong geldings easily carried the men in the saddle as they swam across the deep, narrow river.

Although neither of them admitted it, the jogging of their horses caused them a lot of discomfort in the right shoulder. Again without ever mentioning it, they had the worry that since they were both right-handed, their gun hands had to be badly affected by the dull pain of their wounds.

While they were stopped at an arroyo to water their horses, Doc understood when Raider suddenly went for his revolver and blasted off two shots at a small boulder about forty yards away. Both bullets knocked flakes off the stone. Raider seemed relieved.

They looked for and found landmarks Caballito had told them about, and a little way into the foothills they came to an adobe house. Children were herding sheep to an area of grass in the bare red rock. The door of the house was open, but it was too dark inside to see in.

"Hello," Doc called out, without dismounting.

A thin, middle-aged Mexican with a rifle stood in the doorway.

"Señor Sanchez?"

"*Sí.*"

"*Habla Inglés?*"

"*Sí.*"

"Great. Please let El Caballito del Diablo know that two men who made a promise to him outside Williamville came by to keep that promise. He can find us at the Dunwell ranch, just west of the Tumbling K, on the other side of the Pecos."

"*Sí.*"

The man went back in the house, and Raider and Doc turned their horses about and rode slowly away.

"He could have offered us a drink of water," Raider complained. "Still, we're not doing too badly on our first day out."

"I hope that telegram is there when we get back to town," Doc said. "We can take Judith and my wagon to the ranch. I got a feeling we're going to need Caballito out there."

Raider asked, "You think that Mexican understood what you told him in English?"

"*Sí.*"

"You got no proof it was McClintock," Sheriff Jackson Dean pointed out to Doc and Raider. "I believe you when you say it was him who shot you and so will most other folks, but it's still just your word against his. And you can bet he will deny it."

"But he ended up with the body of Crazy Joe Fields," Raider said.

"In collecting the bounty at San Carlos," Dean replied, "McClintock said he came across Crazy Joe riding alone in the brush and they had a shoot-out. There's nothing to show it wasn't Crazy Joe who shot you two up and then got himself hit later by Mournful John."

"That's not the way it happened," Raider growled.

"So *you* say," the sheriff snapped back. "Now if you boys insist, I'll ride out to the Tumbling K and accuse McClintock. He's still in the county and in my jurisdiction. If he confesses, I'll arrest him. If he denies it, I'll ride back to town empty-handed."

"Forget it," Raider said grudgingly.

"We just want it to be on the record that we asked for your assistance," Doc said.

"And didn't get it," Raider added.

"It's on the record, gentlemen," the sheriff responded coldly. "It might also interest you to know that Noah Blake was in here trying to get me to arrest Will Tucker and other small ranchers on murder evidence equally as flimsy as yours."

Raider and Doc stood and picked up their hats. Outside the cool sheriff's office, the late afternoon sun blazed down in the street.

"Bed rest sure wrecks a man," Raider muttered. "After that horseback ride out to the Mexican, all my bones are shook asunder. I don't even like to think of trekking out to the Dunwell ranch on your wagon. That damn fool mule of yours likes to drop the wagon wheels in every hole she can find."

Doc bristled at this insult to Judith. "You can walk alongside her if you prefer."

"I'd be afraid of leaving you both too far behind."

Next morning both Raider and Doc woke up sore as hell from their exertions of the day before. A telegram from Chicago had authorized their move to the Dunwell ranch, and now they looked out the windows at rolling pastures instead of the dusty main street of Williamville. A dozen fine horses stood in the nearest corral. Bacon sizzled as Will Tucker prepared breakfast on the stove.

"What you boys want to start out at?" Tucker asked.

"It'd be a good idea for us to get the lay of the land," Raider said. "Ride down first along this stream to the other small ranches, and then back along the ridge that marks the boundary with the Tumbling K."

Doc nodded his agreement.

"I still can't get over that old telegram coming in just like that," Tucker said as he served them eggs, bacon, sourdough bread, and coffee. "Sure great to have two Pinkerton agents sitting here on our side."

It occurred to Doc that Will Tucker was not as naive a country boy as he was pretending. Having two Pinkertons on their side was a master stroke for the small ranchers in one way, in that it gave legitimacy to their cause. Now they could no longer be run over, intimidated, and dispossessed without the world outside becoming aware of it.

"I want someone to guard the ranch house while we're out of it," Doc told Tucker.

"There's two steady ranch hands here. They live in the bunkhouse other side of the corral. One will be staying about the place all day. The other will keep his eye on the cattle along with us volunteer ranchers who are helping the widow."

The valley was almost completely clear of thorny scrub except for some rocky hollows and dips. The long, rich grass here reminded Raider more of Wyoming than Texas. They came to the stream, which was less than a foot deep and so narrow at this point a horse could leap it and keep his hooves dry. But down in this arid part of Texas, this little stream that flowed all year round was worth killing for.

The ranch was small by Texas standards, yet it took three hours to ride to its southern boundary, which consisted of the valley narrowing as two ridges came together in a V, cut at its point by the passage of the stream. On the other side of the ridges the terrain was flat, with thorny scrub and prickly pear, except along both sides of the stream, which created a ribbon of vibrant green through the gray flatness of sunbaked soil. The heat caused things to shimmer before their eyes. Dust rose high in the air above men working with cattle in makeshift pens a little way off.

"Come over and I'll introduce you," Tucker said, leading the way on his horse.

When they got there the men were too busy for talk, and they waited till their work was finished. As they watched, the men worked in teams on calves about three months old. One lively bull calf was roped. One man grabbed its front ankles in one hand and its ears in the other, while a second man grabbed its tail and a rear leg. Together they upended the calf onto its right side. The first man held the animal's head to the ground with his knee on its neck and pulled forward on one foreleg and pressed back on the other. The second man sat in the dust behind the calf's rump, pulling back on the beast's top rear leg and using a boot to push forward on its under leg.

Unable to put its legs beneath it, the calf lay helplessly on its side, its breath coming in quick bursts through its flared nostrils flecked with foam and its eyes wide with fear. It gave a low bleating call to its mother.

A third man walked from another calf pinned on the ground to this one. He carried a thin-bladed knife in his right hand. His left hand reached between the calf's rear legs and caught its scrotal sac. Stretching the sac to its full extent, he cut across its lower end. His fingers reached in and pulled out one long yellow testicle, which he cut from its connecting cord. Then the other. He stood upright again and, on his way to the next calf, threw the two testicles onto the fire in which the branding irons were heating.

Through the dust and heat, they watched a fourth man pull a branding iron from the hot coals. The end of the iron was bright red, and the man held it to the earth to cool it off. He held his palm in front of the brand to test its heat. Shaking the iron to rid it of dirt and ash, he strode to the calf and carefully positioned the iron above the animal's hide before making contact with the hot brand. He held the brand against the calf's left hip for a little longer than a second, just long enough for it to scorch through the hair and indelibly mark the hide. The calf bawled.

As the branding iron was returned to the fire, a fifth man approached the calf. He too held a knife in his right hand. He bent the calf's left ear in two and, with two cuts, removed a diamond-shaped piece from its center.

Then the two men pinning the calf to the ground released their holds. The beast struggled upright and stood bewildered, a bit unsteady on its legs.

"Nice clear brand," Tucker remarked, looking at the red weal in the shape of a vertical numeral 21 on the calf's left hip. "Good old Standing Twenty-one. You know, if those boys holding the calf down let it twitch, you could end up with a lazy or tumbling twenty-one, depending on which way it leans. Got to be real careful about that. You often see brands blurred, too, when the branding iron hasn't been held firm enough. But this one's a beauty, and not too deep either, so there won't be no scabs or infection setting in. In a couple of days, calf won't know it's there."

One of the men chased the calf out of the work pen into a larger holding enclosure in which the cut and marked calves were being returned to their mothers. As this calf wandered in, a cow approached and sniffed it under the belly and chin, then rejected it. Other cows came up to the calf and sniffed it also, looking for the scent of their own calves, and shouldered it away or waved a long horn at it when they discovered it was not theirs.

Suddenly the calf ran partway across the enclosure to one particular cow, which in turn ran forward to meet it. The cow sniffed the calf and then began to lick the hair of her newfound offspring's neck and sides. The calf nuzzled up to its mother, and she continued grooming it until she came to the empty sac that had once swelled with testicles. She sniffed the miserable remnant. When a cowhand walked nearby, she lowered her horns and moved at him menacingly.

As the work finished, the dust settled. One of the men at the fire beckoned to Tucker, Doc, and Raider with his knife.

"Help yourself to some desert trout," he said, indicating the calf testicles roasting on the hot coals. "Pick them out on a knife blade. The ones that have burst open are cooked just right."

Doc and Raider had gained a good idea of the layout of the small ranches by the time a rider galloped over a nearby rise of land and loosed two pistol shots in the air.

"He needs help fast," Will Tucker said, and spurred his horse. As Doc and Raider galloped alongside him, he shouted, "Two shots is our signal to drop everything and come quick. We figure we can raise a dozen men in less than an hour with a single rider."

They caught up with the rider who had shot the pistol twice. "It's Jim Prendergast's place. The hired guns chased Jim home and have surrounded his ranch house. I knew you was with these two Pinkertons and came to get you. You want me to ride on and get others? There's seven or eight of those hired guns around that ranch house."

"No, you come with us," Doc told him, as they gathered speed. "Did they see you leave to get help?"

"I was off to one side when they came chasing Jim over the range. No one saw me."

"Let's go!" Raider yelled impatiently.

The four men galloped the dry flat land, raising a great plume of dust in their wake.

They slowed their horses and followed a draw that brought them close to the sound of shots but kept them out of sight. They left the draw where they had the cover of some big rocks. From there they could see the house, and in the foreground men stretched full length firing rifles at it. The attackers formed a crescent, as if they wished to leave plenty of room for those in the house to escape. One man stayed back with seven horses behind a small hill. The other six emptied their rifles into the house, reloaded, and fired again.

Answering fire was returned from the house, and this kept the attackers at a distance.

"I reckon I see five riflemen inside that ranch house," Raider said.

"I don't know who they are, then," Will Tucker responded. "Jim Prendergast is the only grown man living there."

Raider indicated the leftmost attacker, who was more or less isolated from the rest. "Why don't Will and I take this one while you two see what you can do about chasing off their horses? Then we'll have them trapped on foot on open ground."

Doc and the other rider pulled away along a low ridge. In the fury of the shooting, Raider and Will rode up undetected behind the rifleman they had selected. Still hidden among the rocks, they dismounted and watched him. Across the flat land between the gunman and the house, four white chickens ran in panic. The rifle recoiled in the gunman's hands and one chicken was splayed in midair in a cloud of its white feathers before flopping, dead or wounded, to the ground.

"These bastards are doing it for sport!" Will Tucker snarled and moved forward out of the cover of the rocks.

Raider went with him, and they walked up behind the prone gunman who was now plugging away at the windows of the house. Raider would have preferred if all four of them had split up, but it went unsaid between him and Doc that they couldn't depend on these untried ranchers in a firefight—thus Raider had taken one and Doc the other. Raider and Will themselves drew shots from the defenders in the house. Will waved to them, and they stopped shooting in their direction. The rifleman twenty yards in front of them still had no notion he was being approached from behind.

"Hey, you!" Raider said in a casual tone.

The rifleman twisted about, fast as a polecat, but before he could swing his barrel around to bear on Raider, he found himself looking into the black, unwinking eye of a .30-.30 caliber carbine.

"Throw it well away from you." The man bared his teeth, but he threw the rifle a dozen feet from himself. "Now your revolver." The man obeyed. Raider turned to Will Tucker. "Keep him covered here. I'll go see if the others need a hand. If this one makes a sudden move, don't wait to see what he has in mind—just give him a quick bullet in the gut."

Will nodded and covered the gunman lying on the ground with his rifle.

Raider turned away to go back to get his horse among

the rocks. As soon as he turned his back, the gunman, aware that in Will Tucker he was no longer covered by a skilled gunfighter, pulled a sawed-off double-barreled shotgun from beside him in the long grass. He flicked back one hammer and discharged the right barrel at Will and Raider. Will cringed from the expected blast and his rifle shot went wide. The buckshot knocked him flat on the ground.

Raider was farther away and felt the stings—the multiple needles of pain—as the scattering shot hit his back. With the impact of the shot and the sound of the blast, Raider's right hand dropped automatically to the handle of his Remington .44 revolver. The carbine cradle over his left arm would have been much slower. His body twisted as his six-gun left its holster with his right thumb pulling back the hammer.

The gunman peered at them through the haze of blue smoke from his previous shot and pulled back the hammer of the left barrel with his left fingers. His big mistake was to wait to bring his left hand back on the stock for a two-handed grip on the shotgun. He should have loosed off with one hand and aimed low enough to allow for the greater recoil.

Raider's bullet caught him to one side of his Adam's apple and tore half his throat away clear to his spinal bone. The gunman stood erect for a moment, looked too surprised to pull the trigger of the shotgun, then fell stiffly sideways.

Will Tucker sat up. His face was dotted with red pimples caused by the shot, so that he looked like a teenaged boy.

"Your eyes all right?" Raider asked.

"Yes," he said unsteadily.

"Lucky."

"I'm sorry, Raider. I let you down."

"You let yourself down worse since you took it in the face. If that shotgun barrel hadn't been sawed off and caused the shot to scatter real early, you'd be chopped-up meat right now."

Will Tucker nodded contritely. "Next time I'll listen when you say shoot."

"The shooting's stopped. Let's ride down to the ranch house and let them pick these lead pellets out of our skins."

They walked back to their horses. Raider put his foot in the stirrup, swung his leg over the horse's back, and came down heavily in the saddle. He moaned and cursed.

"What's wrong?" Tucker asked, concerned.

"I just sat down on some of that buckshot."

CHAPTER SEVEN

Raider stood looking out the front window of Jim Prendergast's ranch house. Broken glass crunched under his boots. Jim's children were chasing an armadillo. The little animal, with its inquisitive nose and bands of heavy armor, deliberately allowed the children to almost trap it before it would suddenly leap a foot in the air, twist about, run between one child's legs, and zigzag across the open ground with all of them chasing it and shouting, "The 'diller! The 'diller! He's getting away!"

Finally the armadillo stopped, rooted feverishly in the gray dirt, buried its head—and stayed put. The children poked it a few times but soon lost interest in a plaything that was this stupid. They wandered away. And the armadillo stayed as he was.

"It's hard to believe it was only you, your wife, and those four kids shooting back from inside the house," Raider said to Prendergast, a small, mild-looking man with a faraway look in his hazel eyes.

"I think it was Betty here who done most of the shooting." He patted his short, dumpy wife on the shoulder. "If you boys hadn't come along, she might have wiped them out."

They all laughed at this, except Will Tucker. Up to this, Will had prided himself on being the hardest and fastest of the small ranchers. Now he had failed in the first test put to him, and nearly caused both himself and Raider to be killed. On top of this, he had to swallow the fact that meek and mild Jim Prendergast and his wife and kids had held off six professional gunmen. Those kids playing with an armadillo had behaved better than him!

The gunman holding the horses had fired warning shots to alert his buddies of Doc and the rancher's approach. The men had given up their siege and mounted their horses. Doc kept out of rifle range and was satisfied to see them ride off the spread. Then he and the rancher had ridden back to the Prendergast house and cracked jokes as Raider and Tucker had the buckshot picked from their skins with the tip of a fine knife blade.

Betty Prendergast insisted on feeding everyone steak and beans, washed down by huge mugs of strong coffee. While they were eating at the big table near the stove, the four children rushed in to raise the alarm.

"Quick, Paw, the guns!" the oldest boy yelled, grabbing a rifle from where it stood against the wall. "There's an Injun out there!"

"He looks mean as hell," a small girl volunteered, and she also reached for a rifle.

Doc stood between them and the door. "Hold it. Let me take a look."

He and Raider picked up their long guns and went through the door.

El Caballito del Diablo sat on a big roan stallion. He smiled and said, "I heard the sound of much shooting a while back. I thought I might find you here."

"Come in and have something to eat," Doc said.

Caballito hesitated. "These people are no friends of mine."

Doc shrugged. "Since you'll be riding over their land if you want to reach Mournful John McClintock, you might as well get to know some of them now as then. But please yourself."

The Comanche muttered something, dismounted, and gave the huge roan to Prendergast's oldest boy, who stood staring hostilely at the Indian, clutching a rifle by its stock.

"Be careful," the Indian told the boy. "This horse bites white men."

Caballito smiled at the others as the youth and the stallion eyed each other warily and edged along toward the stables.

Inside the ranch house Doc and Raider discovered that the welcome and cheer they had received before were now replaced by a tense silence and watchfulness. When Doc went to introduce the Comanche, he was cut off by Will Tucker's short statement: "We know who he is." Doc ignored this and introduced Prendergast, his wife, and Tucker to Caballito, who ignored them. Betty wordlessly served him steak and beans and coffee while Doc got around to some realities as he saw them.

"Look, I don't give a damn what you folks feel about one another—you don't have room for such luxuries now." Doc looked each of the two ranchers in the eye. "You're fighting for survival, and you've hired us to help you.

Caballito here has his own private quarrel with Mournful John. That puts him for now on the same side as you. Raider and I need him badly. So do you. Forget your differences for now. Caballito goes anywhere he pleases and gets all the help he needs from all of you.''

''All right,'' Will Tucker agreed. ''I'll speak to the others.''

Jim Prendergast nodded in reluctant agreement.

''More coffee?'' his wife asked Caballito by way of a peace offering.

Caballito nodded but otherwise ignored the peacemaking proceedings. When Will Tucker began to officiously explain to him how to get to the Tumbling K from where they were, the Indian silenced him with a cold stare.

''I know the way,'' Caballito said. ''This is all Comanche land.''

The spare bunkhouse at Noah Blake's Tumbling K Ranch, normally used only when extra hands were hired for the spring and fall roundups, was open these days to any drifter who happened by. Whoever stayed was fed and made welcome. No one had to mention that in these parts dead rustlers were worth three hundred dollars a head. Word had been spread far and wide on that. Some of the men rested themselves and their horses a day or two, washed their clothes, played some cards, and drifted on with a full belly. Others showed up periodically, alternating their stays with stopovers in Williamville or other towns and visits to other large holdings that followed the same policy as the Tumbling K. A few stayed on all the time, enjoying a life of indolence and shooting an occasional suspicious character —sometimes another visiting gunman—in order to collect a three-hundred-dollar bounty. The most successful of these was Mournful John McClintock.

Noah Blake laid down only one rule. These men were to stay away from his ranch house and were not to approach any member of his household. To ensure that this rule was obeyed, Blake payed Mournful John an extra fifty dollars a week and gave him the use of an assistant foreman's cabin, separate from the spare bunkhouse.

Blake's foreman kept an eye on things to make sure that normal work on the ranch was not interrupted by the presence of the gunmen. The foreman warned the cowhands to keep away from the drifters, and most of them did. They too could collect the bounty on any rustler they killed and regarded the professional gunslingers as unfriendly and unfair competition for the prize money.

The only troubles so far had been quarrels among the drifters themselves, and no one on the ranch intervened in these disputes. With no booze, no women, and little money, the men had no good cause to fight except out of irritation with each other. And out in these wide-open spaces, no one felt cooped up or crowded in with others, so things were peaceful enough, all things considered.

Noah Blake, careful always to show himself as a landowning gentleman of good family and fine breeding, even in these rough surroundings and crude company, was not above consorting with the lower orders when it was to his advantage to do so. He found it very much to his advantage to stop by to chat with Mournful John McClintock. As well as keeping on friendly terms with this cold-blooded bounty hunter, Blake had to admit a certain fascination with this melancholic man who obviously respected nothing and no one in this world or the next. That alone would not have made McClintock unusual in this part of Texas. What interested Blake was that McClintock was a thinking man who could analyze his own thoughts and those of others, who could have led an easier, safer life without much effort—and who perhaps once had. Blake noted that Mournful John never let down his reserve, never relaxed in the company of others, that everything he did was calculated, grim, predetermined. . . .

Blake and McClintock sat in old woven straw chairs on the little porch of the assistant foreman's cabin. The sun set behind a purple bar of cloud and sent red, pink, and gold washes over the evening sky that created an atmosphere of peace and fulfillment.

"Sure, I agree that the rustling has dropped off since we set the bounty," Blake was saying, "but that warning will wear thin, mark my words. They'll be back here just as soon as they reckon the first wave of hotshot bounty hunters will have become bored and moved on."

McClintock stretched his legs contentedly. "I'm not complaining, Mr. Blake."

"I know that, Mr. McClintock. The point I'm making is that we shouldn't lose our momentum after a good start. We've made a great beginning. Now we have to keep the effort up."

"You're only going to keep these gunfighters around while they can make money," Mournful John said in a bored voice. "No rustlers, no money, no more bounty hunters."

"I realize that. I thought perhaps you could persuade them to bide their time and they would be duly rewarded."

"It's no concern of mine, Mr. Blake, what these riffraff choose to do."

They were distracted by the sound of shouting from the spare bunkhouse, thirty yards from them. Figures crossed back and forth in front of an oil lamp in the bunkhouse window. Finally two men spilled out of the doorway, thrusting at each other with bowie knives. Neither wore a gunbelt—probably they were buddies who would make peace again after some abuse and some wild stabs not really meant to hit home.

However, one man seemed either not to know how to thrust and parry with a bowie or he had already received an injury that impaired his ability to fight. He backed down before the increasing ferocity of his opponent, whose blood lust was roused by his increasing success in the quarrel.

In a gleam of sunset, Blade and McClintock could see the beads of sweat on the winning man's forehead and the fixed look in his eyes as he stooped and held his blade at an angle before him. He stalked the other, who faltered backward before him, a step at a time.

Noah Blake looked mildly annoyed by this, like a proper easterner who has just seen a neighbor's dog root in his flower bed.

Then they saw the man backing away stumble and right himself. His assailant was upon him, punching at his eyes and throat with the broad blade, which could chop into human flesh the way an ax head could be buried into green sapwood. The man put up his left hand to shield his eyes, and the point of the bowie pierced his palm. He blocked repeated thrusts of the knife blade with his open hand until it was a slivered bloody stump and not enough to withstand the murderous attacks any longer.

One vicious thrust in his side finished everything. The

broad blade was held flat to fit between the slats of the ribs, was buried in his body up to its hilt, was drawn out as his body collapsed on the ground, and was wiped, first one side and then the other, on his denim vest to rid the bright steel of his life's blood.

Still clutching the knife before him, the victor turned away and went into the bunkhouse. He emerged again a few moments later with his rifle, gunbelt, sleeping roll, and saddlebags and headed for the stables. He ignored the body of the man he had stabbed, still feebly thrashing in the dust.

"Damn." Blake got to his feet. "I'll have to send someone to fetch the sheriff at first light tomorrow."

Mournful John looked up from rolling a cigarette in his left hand. "Better watch one of us don't drag in that corpse and demand a three-hundred-dollar bounty from you."

He laughed mirthlessly.

Sarah Cooper was saddling a horse in the stables when the gunman came in. She stayed quietly in the stall and hoped he wouldn't notice her. She watched as he cleaned his bowie knife on a handful of hay, strapped on his gunbelt, lifted his saddle from a trestle, and put it on his horse. In three minutes he was riding out. Sarah was unaware of the fight and didn't trouble to wonder where the gunman was going in the gathering dusk.

She hurried at her task, and a few minutes later she too rode away—unnoticed, she hoped, by anyone at the ranch. Since coming to Texas, she had ridden almost every day. The horse knew her and responded to her commands. Riding side-saddle, she cantered across the open land to the dark form of the ridge on the Tumbling K's western boundary. She had to get to the ridge and find her way through the draw while it was still twilight. Once she was through the draw, she would have the lights in the Dunwell ranch house in the distance to guide her.

It never occurred to Sarah Cooper that there might be no lights in the Dunwell ranch house to guide her and that she would find herself alone on a ridge in the dark and too far away to return to the Blake ranch house. She was much more concerned over what Doc Weatherbee's reaction would be to her unexpected arrival. She knew how men could be when women displeased them. And here she was, only a short while ago a very proper lady resisting Raider's advances, riding out alone at night across the range into the arms of her lover. At least so she hoped. She was too preoccupied with these thoughts to notice a man on horseback, standing still in a shadowy hollow, training a rifle on her.

His ears had picked up the sound of the horse's hooves during one of the times he had stopped to listen and look into the fading light behind him for signs of pursuit. He had pulled his rifle from the saddle scabbard and was ready to draw a bead when the figure rode out of the gloom. A woman riding sidesaddle! He recognized her— the Blake children's governess. Pretty woman but a snob. No time for the likes of him. He kept her in the rifle sights as she rode by not far away without seeing him. Having waited to see if she was being tailed by someone else and satisfied that she wasn't, he rode after her himself.

He grinned like a hungry fox. It was almost dark, but it might not be such a lonely night for him alone in his bedding on the open range after all. As soon as he figured out what she was up to, he would grab her and enjoy her. Meanwhile his native caution urged him to just tag along and see what was happening first.

Passage through the draw in the ridge, which she had heard repeated many times in the Blake house as the easiest way onto the Dunwell spread, was slow. She let her horse have his head in the almost complete darkness, left it to him to navigate his way around big rocks and stumble till he had found firm footing. Stones clattered now and then behind her, almost as if a second rider was following stealthily behind her—but she dismissed this as her woman's nervousness and resolved to pay attention only to what was ahead till she saw those saving beacons, the lights in the Dunwell ranch house windows. Doc would be there . . . and hopefully he would be pleased by her surprise visit. Sarah prayed she was not making a big mistake.

He knew now where the governess was going. A traitor in Blake's own household! Riding out to meet the enemy at night! The identity of that spy would be worth five times the price of a dead rustler to Noah Blake. He could have caught up with her easily in the draw, knocked her from her horse, and enjoyed her body to his heart's content—if it hadn't been for the money. In order to collect that, he would have to let her ride to the Dunwell ranch house and then ride back to the Blake ranch at first light in the morning.

Unless she was running away and never coming back! Then he should pounce on her flesh right now and enjoy himself while he had the chance. But she didn't have to run, like him. She could go anytime she chose. No, she would ride back at dawn, having given the enemy the information he needed. Maybe her lover . . .

Fifteen hundred dollars. He would ask Noah Blake to pay that to find out who the spy was. Now that he was on the run because of that dumb bastard he had killed outside the bunkhouse, he could use the money to ride clean away. Maybe up to Wyoming. No one knew him there. Or California. Why not? The governess was pretty, but she sure as hell wasn't worth fifteen hundred. With that kind of cash he could have a score of women prettier than her. He could have them in twos and threes if he wanted to. He would let her go. . . .

Sarah had hardly asked herself why she was going to see Doc—her physical need to be with him was enough for her. She had no information to give him or the small ranchers—she had already told him all she knew when she brought the news that Mournful John was on the Tumbling K. McClintock in turn now knew that the two Pinkerton agents were on the next spread to him—and a war of nerves had begun, she supposed. She could never understand why men got into such things!

At last she saw the lighted windows of the Dunwell ranch house. In rising expectation mixed wtih girlish shyness, she urged her horse across the soft grass.

The gunfighter tied his horse to a railing of a corral where it was in total darkness. He then eased his way along toward the house, keeping out of the rectangles of light cast on the ground by the windows. He needed to see who the governess was talking to. The two Pinkertons that the small ranchers had hired were based here, that was common knowledge. But for his story to stick, he would need to actually see the governess talking to one of them. That would be something Blake could not deny.

The gunfighter had no way of knowing that Noah Blake not only was aware of Sarah's liaison with Doc Weatherbee but was quite happy with it, since it kept Doc away from the blond Adele. Blake just made sure nothing of significance was ever said opposite the governess, which was not difficult, because a gentleman like himself was brought up to keep ladies in ignorance.

In one brightly lit window the gunfighter recognized the big Pinkerton with the mustache. He was playing cards at a table with two of the small ranchers. The governess must be talking to the one in fancy eastern clothes. There was no one in the next lighted room. The gunman crept along the side of the building to where a dim glow came from between two drapes drawn partway across the inside of a window. He peered in, and in the soft glow of the turned-down oil lamp saw the governess stretched on the bed with the second Pinkerton. That was all he needed. . . .

Yet he paused to watch. For the hell of it. He gazed in at Doc's busy hands fondling her body. It had been some weeks since he'd had any himself, and he felt himself grow stiff as he looked on at another man's pleasure. That could have been his. Had he not been greedy for money. His concentration was so intense that he was startled by a loose horse that wandered close to him out of the darkness —it had probably come in out of the range looking for water, he thought, and peered in through the window again.

Next he heard a slight hiss close to his boots. Snakes didn't come out at night. He looked down and saw that the large loop of a lariat had fallen over him and that its noose was tightening about his ankles. He saw the rope tauten over the back of the stray horse, being pulled by someone concealed on the other side of the animal.

As his feet went from beneath him, he saw a hand grab the mane of the horse, then an Indian pull himself up to ride the animal bareback and without reins. The Indian looped the end of the lariat once about the top of the horse's shoulders, dug his heels in its sides, and began to tow the gunfighter by his ankles over the rough dusty ground.

The gunman's body felt the sickening jolts, and his legs felt as if they were being ripped from his hip sockets. His right hand groped for his revolver, but it had already been knocked out of its holster. If he could get out his bowie, he could cut the lariat dragging him mercilessly over the ground. The dust tore at his skin like sandpaper, and sharp pebbles and roots gouged into his flesh. He pulled the bowie from its sheath and held it up so it would not be knocked from his hand. He tried to ignore the pain and to double his body forward so he could reach with the blade to the rope about his ankles.

It was no use! Each time, he summoned every ounce of strength he had, but his ankles were cruelly jerked forward and his head and shoulders fell backward. When he knew he no longer had the strength to try again, he threw the knife at the back of the Indian riding the horse. He saw its blade catch starlight for a second as it arced toward its target. The knife flew wide of its mark. He had nothing left to do now except plead for mercy. . . .

He shouted as the skin on his butt, back, and elbows was scraped to pieces by the abrasive soil. For a moment the gunfighter thought his ordeal was over as he lay unmoving in the dust, yet when he looked he saw that the Indian was tying the end of the lariat to the saddle pommel of the gunfighter's own horse, which he had loosed from the corral rail. The Indian whacked the horse, and then the gunfighter was dragged off across the ground, his body turning over and over like bait on the end of a fishing line.

Dust on his tongue and the inside of his mouth choked the man's cries of pain, dirt caked his open eyes, clay absorbed his oozing blood. . . . He looked scarcely human and was only barely alive when El Caballito del Diablo gave the horse a final crack on its haunches and sent it galloping in total darkness over the sharp rocks of the draw in the ridge that led to the Tumbling K.

Sarah had insisted first that she had seen something through the window and then that she had heard a noise of something being dragged. Doc had indulged her whims by getting up to pull the drapes closed. Her returned to the bed with a tolerant smile. He had neither seen nor heard a thing. Women!

He lay beside her on the bed again and fondled her body and removed her clothes, item by item. Doc sucked in one creamy smooth tit and rolled the nipple with his tongue. His mouth felt the nipple harden and swell.

He slid his hand down her writhing stomach and felt her tense expectantly as his fingers stroked her curly brown bush. Her clit peeked out at him from her juicy slit.

He teased the erectile nub of her clit with a fingertip, and her whole body trembled as he sent waves of pleasure through her.

Doc raised his mouth from her tit, along her neck to her luscious mouth. He licked her lips, tongue, teeth—thrust his tongue inside her mouth and met hers.

His finger moved from her clit into her cunt and excited her inner lips till her body seethed beneath his touch.

"Come into me! Quick!" she begged.

Doc mounted her and sank his shaft into her welcoming depths. He rammed his cock into her till she came in a series of little yelps, clutching at him feverishly, culminating in one long howl that would have done any coyote proud beneath the moon.

She held him fiercely in her legs while he delivered his pent-up manhood juices into the crevice of her trembling flesh.

CHAPTER EIGHT

Doc Weatherbee rode back alone after seeing Sarah Cooper to within sight of the Tumbling K ranch house. He had half expected to be chased off by some of Blake's gunmen, but he saw no one. Back in the valley he spotted Raider and Will Tucker setting out on horseback and decided to join them. So long as Mournful John wished to keep out of their way, he could do so—but only at a loss to his reputation for fearlessness. By now even Noah Blake knew the real purpose of the Pinkertons' presence. Blake's method of fighting back seemed to be a calculated lack of confrontation. This was not a bad ploy, since there was nothing Doc or Raider could do unless some incident justified their trespass onto Blake's land.

Grass grew on the summer pasture slopes of the valley that made up the Dunwell spread, but down in the valley floor the sun had baked the land dry and all the creeks but one. The place was hot, flat, dusty, and treeless. Stunted mesquite shrubs sat atop small sand hills. Precious blades of green grass peeped out of the ground in the shade of tall yuccas.

Doc caught up with Raider and Tucker and let his horse fall into an easy walk alongside theirs. In places they rode through thickets in which prickly pear, cat's claw, mesquite, and yucca tore at their buckskin chaps. In a clearing in one thicket, they came upon a cow and her healthy newborn calf. The mother longhorn's protective instinct was aroused, and she lunged at the nearest horse, hooking upward toward its belly with the tip of her right horn. With the dig of a single spur, Tucker spun the horse with such speed and precision that the cow hooked her deadly horn into empty air, lost her balance, and went down on her two front knees.

Tucker did not change his horse's slow walking pace and did not bother to glance back at the cow, which stood bewildered a moment before returning to her calf.

Raider whistled admiringly at his skill. "These animals are kind of wild down here."

"Sure," Tucker agreed. "That mother cow is about nine years old. She was branded at about three months old, and if she ain't been sick, that's the only time she's ever been handled. When they hide out here in the thickets, we often miss them in the drives. They get wild as buffalo—'cept a longhorn is a lot meaner and smarter."

Raider pointed to a group of vultures slowly descending on something ahead. "Might be that gunman Caballito said he took care of last night. The horse might have shook him free."

Doc shook his head. "Judging by how quiet things were over at the Tumbling K this morning, I'd say they found him over there, like Caballito said they would."

Doc had no way of knowing that Noah Blake had *two* bodies to show the sheriff that morning.

"I think those birds are coming down on one of Dunwell's cattle," Tucker said. "Screwworm, I bet. We've had a good bit of that this year. Some years are worse than others."

"Get in their wounds, don't they?" Raider asked. "You don't see it much farther north."

"No? Well, these screwflies is half the size of my thumbnail"—Tucker showed them—"and bluish green with kind of stripes on them. They lay their eggs in any kind of wound or on the birth cord of a newborn calf. The worms that hatch are shaped like screws and eat their way into the meat. If you find them early enough, a gob of tobacco juice in the wound will kill them. Mostly it's too late when you find them."

They rode on, and Doc and Raider noticed for the first time how many disassembled, sun-bleached bones of cattle lay about them, persisting for years on the hot, dry land.

When they came near to where they had seen the vultures circling, there was no sign of them anymore. They soon saw why. The scavengers were ravening upon the body of a calf. The dead animal's belly was bloated with gases, and its eyes, balls, and asshole had already been torn away by the fierce curved beaks of the huge birds that crawled over the carcass like flies.

"Been dead more than a day," Tucker opined casually, as the gluttonous vultures ignored their presence. "Too late now to tell what he died of."

One big vulture perched on the calf's shoulder, dipped its featherless naked red head and neck into a hole in the animal's side, then pulled its head out with a beakful of decomposing tissues, which it hungrily swallowed.

Doc looked away, reminded of the four men he and Raider had left as carrion outside Williamville.

They rode on. Doc knew they might have many days ahead of them of just wandering about on the range. Out here things happened in their own sweet time. A town man's getting restless made no difference. Besides, Doc noticed that every day he was getting stronger and more fully recovered from his gunshot wound. Which brought him back in a vicious circle to Mournful John McClintock. They had to get him. Soon.

The three men followed the bank of the stream for a time and stopped when they came to a dozen head of cattle staggering about.

Raider dismounted and pulled a small plant with yellow flowers out of the ground. "Here's your trouble." He stamped his boot on another of the plants. Air-filled bladders in the plant burst with loud pops. "Pop-ball loco weed. Leastways they're not on purple loco. That really knocks the shit out of them."

Tucker examined the steers with a practiced eye and shook his head in disagreement. "These ones here eat pop-ball for breakfast. Then purple loco the rest of the day. And they ain't never going to eat nothing else till they die. Look at them stagger! Dunwell must have bought them up-country a ways. We got a lot of loco weed growing here and calves born in these parts hardly ever get on it. Just damn fool animals that come from somewhere else. Hey, look at that crazy one trying to drink!"

One steer stood by the bank of the stream and attempted to drink with its head a yard short of the water. It kept coming up with a tongue coated with sand and a surprised look in its glazed eyes.

Doc said, "Reminds me of Raider when he can't fit his nose in a whiskey glass."

Mournful John McClintock and three gunfighters, looking pleased with themselves, rode behind four men also on horseback whose wrists were tied behind their back with rawhide thongs.

"Wait here," Mournful John told them when they reached the main corral near Noah Blake's ranch house. Acknowledging that he too was forbidden to approach the family home, he called to a cowhand, "Tell Mr. Blake I want to see him."

Mournful John rolled himself a cigarette in his left hand as he waited. When he saw Blake approach, he dismounted and walked to meet him.

"Four of them? What did you bring them in here for?" Blake was questioning why the four men were still alive, but he wouldn't do that openly.

"Caught them rustling by the red butte to the southwest. Rest of them got away, but empty-handed."

Blake was aware his question had not been answered. "Why are they here?"

Mournful John's mouth went crooked. "Warn't no trees out there to hang them."

Blake smiled dutifully at this little joke and waited.

"I know two of 'em," Mournful John went on. "They'd make right good guns for you to have around in exchange for their lives."

"So keep them."

"That would be leaving me and those three men six hundred dollars short for your convenience," Mournful John explained.

"You want me to pay a bounty on them and then hire them?"

"It's up to you."

"We could use them if they're good," Blake conceded. "But they got to earn their bounty back with a dead rustler apiece."

Mournful John nodded and walked back to the corral. He pointed to two of the rustlers and gestured with a finger around his neck. The gunmen swiftly knotted nooses in each of two four-foot lengths of rope and stood on the top rail of the corral to tie the free ends of the ropes to each of the tall poles that marked the gate. With their own horses, they maneuvered the mounts of the two men sideways against the rails and dropped a noose around the neck of each man. Hands bound behind them, the two men sat impassively in their saddles, knowing that no pleas for mercy could help them now, that their time had come, that they must die as they had lived.

"Eeyah!" a gunman yelled, slapping the rumps of the two condemned men's horses simultaneously.

The horses started forward and left their loads behind, each kicking for a while on his length of rope.

Small groups of cowhands stood watching without coming too close. Noah Blake witnessed the scene alone and from a distance.

Mournful John nodded toward the second pair of rustlers, and the three executioners set about cutting two more lengths of rope, tying nooses and knotting them next to the ropes suspending the other two rustlers.

"Damn you, McClintock," one of the rustlers said—a gaunt, hollow-cheeked man with dead eyes. The long fingers of his bound hands curled and uncurled behind his back. "We was friends once. We'd never have done this to you."

"I ain't done nothing to you yet," Mournful John told him.

The two men looked hopefully in his direction, away from their comrades whose heads were set at odd angles on their slack necks and who hung down like long whithered leaves from each tall pole.

"Seeing as we're old friends," Mournful John continued, "maybe I could do something for you two."

Both men waited in silence, the gaunt one with his fingers curling and uncurling and the other with a bullet head and a cast in his left eye. They were not going to beg for their lives.

"Mr. Blake, who owns this here spread," Mournful John told them, "might give you a chance to earn back that bounty he has to pay us for catching you rustling. If I was to put in a good word for you and if you was willing . . ."

"We're willing," the gaunt one said quietly.

"I'm mighty pleased to hear that." But Mournful John's dour face was not wreathed in smiles. "First rustler each of you ketch pays back your own bounty. After that it's three hundred a head or you're free to leave. And you do what I say while you're here."

"Yes."

McClintock pulled out a knife and held it over the gaunt man's rawhide bonds. He paused before cutting. "You and your brother ain't going to disappoint me now, Ned Harris? I'd take that kind of personal."

Ned looked into the cold eyes of the man holding the knife. "I'll stay."

"Me, too," Jake added, straining to free his wrists . . . and hold a gun in his hand once more.

Will Tucker branched off to go to his own spread and said he would see them again sometime the next day. Raider and Doc continued their leisurely way along the stream. They kept in the shade of the cottonwoods by the bank when they could, because the sun was now high and blistering hot. Raider spotted what he thought were some stray motherless calves in a loose thicket and rode after them to do some cowboying on his own. Three pronghorn antelopes fled before his horse.

Doc laughed and shouted, "Rope 'em and brand 'em, Raider!"

They continued on a ways before stopping to eat the hard cheese and sourdough bread they had brought with them. Doc brewed up strong coffee, boiling whole coffee beans in a pot of stream water over a scrubwood fire. Their horses had drunk their fill and were nibbling on grass at the water's edge. The sky was pale blue and empty. Except for the babble of water and the clicking of insects, a tremendous silence had settled over everything.

Therefore it was all the more a total surprise to Raider and Doc when the bull broke from the cover of the thicket, lowered its huge spread of horns, and bellowed and pawed the dirt with its forelegs.

Raider and Doc got slowly to their feet, avoiding sudden movement what might provoke the animal. Watching for a charge, they eased their revolvers from their holsters.

"Move slowly to the left after me," Raider told Doc. "We got to lead it away from the tethered horses. Move slowly now so you don't excite it."

"Damn, I wish we had our rifles."

Raider started moving slowly to the left. When the bull saw him move, it stopped pawing the ground and followed his actions with its bulging bloodshot eyes.

"I think this is the place it comes to drink in the stream," Doc said rapidly. "It thinks we're trying to stop it drinking."

"Why don't you discuss things with it," Raider said testily and moved some more to the left. "Look at that six-foot spread of horn and its massive forehead. This monster could knock a locomotive off the rails."

"Watch out, Raider! It's real light on its feet!"

Raider heeded Doc's warning. The animal's huge shoulders tapered down into skinny hindquarters, and even as it shifted about to watch them, the bulky animal lifted and placed its cloven hooves as daintily and precisely as a goat.

Raider took another step and the bull lumbered a couple of yards toward him, noisily expelling breath through its widened nostrils. It tossed its head in a kind of practice left-right punch with its horn tips, then lowered its head for the final charge.

"Fire!" Raider yelled.

Both squeezed the triggers of their revolvers. The bull didn't even seem to notice the two .38 bullets Doc sent behind and below its left shoulder, where he reckoned the heart would be. Raider got off three .44-caliber lead slugs into the front of the rampaging beast, which seemed to slow it a bit but nothing more.

Raider tried to outrun, then dodge the bull, which scooped him from beneath, carried him upward on the spread of its horns, and tossed him to the ground five yards away like a discarded apple core.

The bull turned in its tracks and bore down on the

fallen man to gore him with the sharp tips of its horns. Raider was too winded and stunned to get up and run. He hardly seemed to know what was happening to him, yet held on tightly to the revolver in his right hand.

Doc emptied his .38 into the murderous brute coming in for the kill, and this time the four slugs counted. The bull winced and delayed for a moment, then staggered. Blood spurted from the bullet holes in its hide. Its eyes found Raider's prone form again, and it walked deliberately toward him. There was nothing Doc could do. It was too late now. The bull lowered the upturned tip of its left horn to hook Raider through the body and lift him into the air.

Raider reached out and touched the bull between the eyes with the muzzle of his .44 Remington revolver. The gun discharged. The bull paused. Raider thumbed back the hammer and squeezed the trigger again. The bull fell to its knees, looked Raider in the eyes for a second, and fell over on its side with a great thump.

Raider got unsteadily to his feet, covered with dust, and picked up his hat.

Doc, reloading the gun, remarked sadly, "Raider, I think you should forget about ranching."

Doc kept an eye on Raider to see how he was faring after being tossed by the bull. He suggested returning to the ranch house a couple of times, but Raider snapped that he was fine. And just to prove it, Raider insisted that they ride farther along the stream than they had originally intended. Otherwise they would never have heard the shots.

They rode in their direction, to the southwest, and soon saw two plumes of dust—one raised by about half a dozen horsemen heading directly for them. The second dust plume was raised by almost twice that number of men giving chase to them. Those in front were shooting wildly at those behind and riding low in the saddle. For maximum speed, the fleeing horsemen were following a cattle trail that wound through the scrub and crossed the stream through a gap in a grove of cottonwoods where Doc and Raider were placed.

"You want to welcome them?" Doc queried Raider with a grin.

"Reckon so."

They parted and went to the nearest trees on either side of the gap in the trees by the stream. Each cut a mark with a knife in a strong slender tree level with the tip of their horses' ears. Raider threw his lariat and Doc caught its end.

The rope lay snaked across the ground between them as they concealed themselves, still mounted, among the cottonwoods on each side of the gap. They could hear the hoofbeats now, getting louder by the second, and they peered through the shimmering heat to try to see the faces of the men approaching. They were strangers. Raider and Doc had no chance to see their pursuers in the dust the lead horses kicked up behind them. The men still twisted about in their saddles to fire upon those chasing them. Bullets shot by those behind flew over the heads in front and splintered twigs in the trees above Doc and Raider's heads.

The horsemen reached the stream crossing at a gallop. Raider met Doc's eyes, nodded once, twice, and—waiting till the first horses were almost level with them—nodded the third time as the signal to raise and tauten the lariat suddenly to the level marked by their knives on the trees. They rapidly twirled the loose ends of the taut lariat several times about the narrow trunks and held on.

The heads of the first four horses passed beneath the

rope, which caught their riders just below their necks, lifting them out of the saddles and throwing them in the dirt. The fifth horse, a huge bay stallion, saw the rope, could not stop, but reared up and came down against it with his chest, snapping it like a spider thread with his fierce power. The rider was unseated.

The sixth and seventh men, a couple of lengths behind, managed to rein in and pull their horses to the side—not realizing there was nothing to stop them from crossing the stream now that the lariat had snapped. They found themselves looking into Doc and Raider's rifle barrels, took the hint, and dismounted.

The fallen men picked themselves up painfully and saw their escape routes into the trees cut off on one side by Doc and on the other by Raider. They might have made a contest of it with their revolvers against the two long guns if it hadn't been for the arrival of the horsemen chasing them. Doc and Raider recognized many of the fifteen horsemen—including their leader, Will Tucker.

"I thought you said you were going home," Raider said to him.

"I was." Will grinned. "Donaldson here"—he indicated one of his fellow riders—"lost about sixty calves to rustlers yesterday. I saw these boys at work on Hobson's spread and managed to sneak away without them seeing me to round up some help. They had to separate the unbranded calves from the mothers, so we had time to catch them red-handed. Except this time they saw us coming and took off. I don't think we'd have caught them without you two boys appearing like you did."

Doc brushed some imaginary dust from a suit lapel and said modestly, "That's what you hired us for."

"You know them?" Raider asked.

"These four are Blake's regular ranch hands," Tucker said. "These three are bounty hunters."

"Seems like they've been corrupting some of the cowboys," Raider observed. "Right, you lot, drop your gunbelts."

There was a moment of tension as they waited for someone crazy enough to try something. None of them were that crazy.

"String 'em up!" Donaldson yelled. "These bastards stole my calves."

"Yeah! Yeah!" a chorus of voices answered. "Hang 'em! Give 'em the rope!"

Raider walked out and stood between the small ranchers and the cattle thieves. "Sure I know this is range justice for rustlers caught in the act, but now that you've hired Pinkerton agents to help you, you're going to have to go by the laws of the land. And those laws say these men have the right to their day in court, no matter what they've done."

There was loud grumbling and protests at this, although none of them actually came forward to challenge the big Pinkerton and his carbine and .44.

"I guess Raider's got a point," Will Tucker opined. "We can do what we want so long as they're not around, but they go by the book. So when they're on the scene, we do it their way. We weren't doing so good before when we was doing things our way. And like I said, we probably wouldn't have caught up on these seven if it hadn't been for these two Pinkertons. So stop cussing and complaining and go find these varmints' horses. We'll bring them into Williamville, wait for a judge to give them a hearing, and hang them there."

CHAPTER NINE

"Noah Blake's on his way here, along with the sheriff and others!" Will Tucker called out in warning from his early morning lookout post on the roof of the Dunwell ranch house.

"*Adiós*," Caballito muttered and in half a minute had grabbed a horse in the corral, slipped a bridle over its head, opened the gate, and ridden off bareback toward the west.

"I hope he doesn't get indigestion," Doc said solicitously. "Interrupting your breakfast and rushing off like that can't be very good for you."

"You can always give him one of your miracle cures when he gets back," Raider said.

"Blake and the sheriff and more are nearly here!" Tucker shouted at them, now standing at the kitchen table and staring amazed at the two Pinkerton agents as they unhurriedly finished their bacon and eggs, cornbread and coffee. He held up his rifle meaningfully. "You want me to hold them off?"

"No," Doc told him, "but you might put more water on the stove. We won't have enough coffee for them all."

Tucker, mystified, went to do what he was told.

Very lightly and a little too casually, Raider asked Tucker, "Is Mournful John McClintock with them?"

"No."

Raider and Doc exchanged glances.

They heard the jingling of harness and horses' hooves as the men dismounted outside.

A voice yelled, "Raider, Weatherbee, come out with your hands up."

Doc called back, "Come in and have some breakfast with us."

The door was kicked in and Sheriff Jackson Dean and three deputies rushed in, shotguns leveled.

Doc pointed with his fork, "Pull up some chairs. Tucker will fetch you coffee. You two, Blake, come on in, we won't bite you."

Blake had been standing outside the door with a superior look on his face. Now his smirk faded, and he stepped inside.

"Mr. Blake here testified that you captured and hung some of his ranch hands yesterday," the sheriff said in offical tones. "I've come to arrest you for murder."

"Sure, we caught seven of his men rustling yesterday afternoon," Doc agreed.

"And hung them?" the sheriff gueried.

"No. We're bringing them in to you to stand trial as soon as we feed them breakfast. All seven are in that back room."

Noah Blake's mouth dropped open in astonishment. He strode disbelievingly to the door Doc had indicated, opened it, and looked in. A mask of rage possessed his handsome features as he saw his seven men sitting on the floor against the walls, arms bound to their sides. He slammed the room door shut and headed for the doorway outside.

"Hold it a minute, Blake," Doc said. "We were going to bring the sheriff out to your place after we had dumped these seven in the town jail, but now that you're here, I see no reason why he should have to make a double journey."

"To my spread?" Blake asked suspiciously.

"Tell us what you have in mind, Weatherbee," the sheriff said, indicating an empty chair to Blake.

But Doc had no intention of saying a thing until he had finished the food on his plate.

Judith had been feeling neglected by Doc over the past few days. She didn't seem to take well to the ranch horses in the corrals and kept to herself. So that if mules could smile, Judith certainly did as she was harnessed up once again to pull the wagon. Doc often claimed that Judith didn't care a fig what sort of work she had to do so long as she got attention. In Raider's opinion, however, Judith's orneriness outweighed any work she did.

"All right, on your feet," Raider told the seven bound men, helping two of the slower ones with a boot in the hind end. "You're traveling by Pullman coach today."

They loaded the seven of them into Doc's medicine wagon. The sheriff, three deputies, Blake, and Tucker accompanied Raider on horseback, while Doc drove the wagon. The two Pinkertons exchanged a grin at the look of discomfiture on Noah Blake's face. He had ridden out that morning, somehow having gotten word his men had been captured, in order to have Doc and Raider arrested for murder, having assumed reasonably enough that the rustlers had been strung up from the nearest tree as usual. Now here he was riding back with the very same lawmen to see if a charge could be lodged against him on his own land.

Raider and the others rode ahead as the wagon slowly negotiated the rocky draw through the ridge. Once on Tumbling K land, they saw almost two dozen of the small ranchers and their sons, armed to the teeth, herding about sixty cows with the Double Bar D brand of Donaldson on their left hips. Donaldson separated from the group and rode up to greet the sheriff with a smile on his face.

"It's not far from here, Jackson," he said. "They've made a temporary corral out of cut branches and such— enough to keep small calves fenced in. It's in a hollow over yonder."

Blake's eyes blazed. "Any unbranded calves you find on my land belong to me. I don't care whether a man is sheriff or whatever, he can't prove otherwise to me."

Sheriff Jackson Dean tried to keep a neutral expression on his face. "Let's go see."

The cows had been traveling reluctantly and silently until they neared the rise in the ground and heard the bawls of calves in a hollow beyond. They called back and their pace quickened. They pushed aside thorn bushes, horsemen, and whatever came between them and their young. The makeshift corral could not withstand these angry mother longhorns, who shredded its barricades with casual flicks of their heads.

A big reunion took place in the dusty hollow as the cows jostled to scent their calves and, having found them, lowed with joy and licked their fur.

"That doesn't prove a damn thing!" Noah Blake told the sheriff.

"To me it does," Jackson Dean replied. "I'm a cattleman's son, and this I know—men lie, cow's don't."

The shortest route to Williamville from where they were ran by way of the Blake ranch house.

"These are our prisoners," Doc told Tucker. "Raider and I will look after them. You go back with the others as they return the cattle and look after things till we get back."

Tucker smiled. "I can see you boys is just dying to get into town for a few hours. It's a lonely, thirsty life out here on the range. That is, if you don't have no family," he added, as if the foregoing did not apply to him.

"Now that you mention it," Doc said and adjusted his derby, "we might stop off for a few brews and small talk with a painted lady or two."

"You coming back to us?" Tucker asked, a little anxious.

"Don't worry about that, Will," Raider put in. "We still got unfinished business here."

"Talking about which," Doc said, "maybe I can arrange a delay at Blake's ranch house—"

"—while I see if Mournful John happens to be home," Raider finished for him.

Doc was as good as his word. When Blake tried to leave them to go in his ranch house, Doc demanded that the sheriff arrest him for rustling.

"You found the stolen stock on his land," Doc insisted.

"That doesn't prove I knew what my men were up to," Blake shouted. "On a huge spread like this—"

"Let me talk to the seven prisoners," the sheriff said.

Time passed as he did so.

The sheriff then had to reason with an insistent Doc that the theft the men were caught doing was separate from the theft of Donaldson's calves that were recovered on the Tumbling K. Because the men were guilty beyond doubt of one theft did not prove them guilty of the other, although in all probability they committed both. However, there was no direct evidence that Blake's employees had stolen the calves found on his land. The seven men had denied all guilt to the sheriff, and had further denied any involvement on Blake's part in their actions.

Jackson Dean was no fool. He went along with Doc's delaying tactics, obviously aware that Raider was off somewhere. So long as Blake remained distracted and infuriated by Doc's charges, the sheriff did not attempt to make a rapid close of the argument by informing Doc that as a Pinkerton agent he knew the law as well as any man and thus was aware he had no case against Blake in a court of law.

Meanwhile Raider had slipped around by the spare bunkhouse. Sarah Cooper had described the separate cabin occupied by Mournful John McClintock, and this Raider now saw, not far from the bunkhouse next to which he stood.

No one was about. He loosened his revolver in its holster and stepped out to quickly close the distance between him and the cabin door. The windows were high and small. There was no way to conceal his approach. At the door he drew his gun, pulled back the hammer, and held it ready. He heaved the door inward suddenly and leveled the gun on anything that moved in the dim light. Nothing moved. The one-room cabin was empty. An empty bed, unmade. Some shirts. Battered saddlebags. Something moved. On the floor. It was thick as Raider's arm. Coiled. Old and mean, with ten or eleven rattles, buzzing . . .

The diamondback struck at him, and Raider threw himself backward. He felt the rap of the snake's bite on the leather of his riding boots, below his right knee, as he crashed heavily on the floor. The fangs did not penetrate the thick leather—he had been lucky this time. But this big old snake was probably smart enough to strike higher the next time. Raider climbed slowly off the floor to his feet, making smooth and easy movements so as not to irritate the snake—he remembered momentarily how this had not been successful with the bull. The rattler was now between him the the door, which had swung closed. His revolver had fallen and was now too close to the reptile for him to reach it. The snake coiled on the floor into a thick, three-foot-long spring, ready to release itself in a deadly movement faster than a man's eye could follow.

The creature's eyes followed him as he slowly reached behind him and pulled his bowie. He gradually brought his right hand up, aimed, and whipped the projectile at the coils. The snake saw the wide steel blade flying through the air and, with incredible speed, struck at it. The diamondback missed with its fangs but saved itself, since its coils were no longer there for the sharp, heavy blade to pin to the floor. The blade now quivered, struck an inch deep in a board, and the snake stretched into its full length and moved sinuously into the center of the floor before coiling again and rattling in a continuous buzz.

Raider backed into a corner. With this lightning-fast, venom-packed snake in the middle of the cabin floor, there was nowhere for him to maneuver. An ax handle leaned in the corner. It was only the handle—the ax head was missing, yet it was the only weapon he could lay his hands on.

He had no idea whether Mournful John had left this

snake as his watchdog or had seen them coming and had guessed they would search his cabin and had just released it. Someone might even have placed it here to kill Mournful John, and he, Raider, was now ironically saving McClintock's life. Raider had a great fear of snakes—not a nameless, childish terror of them, but a dread and respect for rattlesnakes based on his experience of them. He knew how he had to kill this one. Get it to move. And there was only one way to get it to move—force it to strike, miss, and, instead of recoiling immediately for another strike, change its position.

From where the big diamondback now lay coiled on the floor, if angered it could spring at him and bury its fangs deep in his flesh, and finish him off by emptying its poison sacs into him in multiple bites. He dared not make it feel threatened. Yet he had to make it strike. And miss. . . .

He eased his Stetson off his head with his left hand, clutching the ax handle in his right. Holding the hat by the brim, he flicked it toward the snake. The reptile buried its fangs into the crown of the hat in a midair strike that slapped the Stetson to the floorboards between them.

Raider stepped in. The rattler was confused by this advance and retreated to coil and strike again. In order to move it had to stretch its head and tail and generate wavelike movements through its body to get across the floor. While doing this, it couldn't strike at him as easily as when coiled.

Raider brought the ax handle down and snapped its back. He left the big snake tying itself in knots on the floor and closed the door carefully behind him, hoping the diamondback would retain life and rage enough to greet Mournful John on his return.

•   •   •

Doc Weatherbee cursed and fed the fat, succulent leaves of prickly pear one at a time into the wheel housings to lubricate the live-oak wood axles of his wagon, which were groaning under the unaccustomed weight of the seven bound men he was transporting to Williamville. Judith made no protest, seeming to enjoy her work after her rest on the ranch and, before that, in the town stables while Doc was recovering from his gunshot wound. Raider, the sheriff, and his deputies rode escort on the wagon. Noah Blake, with a purposeful look on his face, had ridden ahead of them to Williamville. Their progress was slow, and he would be there a full two hours before them to prepare whatever he had in mind.

They finally arrived in town, hot and dusty. When the seven men had been put behind bars and they had stabled Judith and Raider's horse, they took off for the Horseshoe Saloon at a near run. The first face they recognized inside was that of Noah Blake. The second was Adele's. The big landowner sat at a table with the blonde. He had a satisfied look on his face.

Raider and Doc took the last vacant table, which was close by Blake's. They ordered a bottle of the best bourbon in the house. Doc had carefully brushed down his suit and tended to his appearance. Raider looked exactly like he felt—dusty, hot, thirsty from hours in the saddle.

Doc's critical eye was roving. "I wonder when that sloe-eyed beauty showed up in town."

It was easy for Raider to see who Doc was talking about. She was tall and thin and being given a hard time by a bunch of penniless wise-asses at the bar.

"She's the purtiest gal in the saloon," Raider opined.

"No," Doc disagreed. "Finest woman here is that blonde with Noah Blake."

"Adele? She's a bitch, Doc. She quit coming to see you after only a few visits when you was hurt."

Doc smiled. "I guess that's because there was nothing I could do for her, the way I was."

"I don't think a woman like that—" Raider stopped. He laughed. "I get it. You just want to take her off Noah Blake. Don't matter a damn if she had wire spectacles and pimples."

"In that case I'd leave her with him," Doc said, rising to his feet and crossing over to the sloe-eyed beauty.

Her name was Linda Sue and she was of the opinion, in a strong Georgia accent, that she would be very pleased to join Doc and his friend at their table. One of the wisecrackers at the bar was about to make a remark until Doc stopped before him so he could hear it real good. After that they watched their manners so far as Linda Sue was concerned.

If Raider hadn't known Doc's tricks, he would have been plain embarrassed to have been sitting at that table with the way Doc flirted and paid compliments to her and said she was that rarest flower of womanhood, a Southern belle. Hell, Raider was from Arkansas, and he hated to hear a Northerner like Doc talk this folderol. But he was curious to see how things would turn out and went along with the setup, even so far as to agreeing with Doc that the skin of Linda Sue's bare shoulders reminded him, too, of a magnolia petal.

With an occasional sidelong glance, Raider could see that Adele was burning with jealousy. Doc never looked once in her direction. He didn't have to. Adele tried to get Noah Blake to fuss over her, but he was preoccupied and unaware of any games being played. She tossed her blond curls in rage and couldn't keep her eyes off Doc's antics with the Southern belle.

When Doc rose from the table unexpectedly and walked alone to a window to gaze out into the street, Adele did not hesitate. Without bothering to excuse herself to Noah Blake, she elegantly strode on her high heels to join Doc.

Blake's mouth hung open in shock and dismay. When he saw Doc and Adele leave, arm in arm, through the batwing doors, his mouth clamped shut and he stared hard at the drink gripped tightly in his right fist.

The clerk at the Hotel Williamville was pleased to provide them with a room. He asked Doc with a straight face, "How long do you expect to be staying with us this time, sir?"

"About an hour."

In the room Adele lost no time by being coy. She peeled off her gown with practiced ease. She wore nothing beneath it. Doc looked at the contours of her breasts, the smooth curving line of her belly, her shapely thighs. . . .

Adele was a real woman. She knew how to give her body wholly to a man. Doc patiently and passionately worked her into a frenzy of lust and then drove the full length of his shaft into her hungering depths.

Raider was still talking to Linda Sue at the table in the Horseshoe Saloon when Noah Blake stalked out—and was still talking to her when Sheriff Jackson Dean came to tell him that Blake had posted bond for the seven men in his jail, having previously arranged by telegraph with a judge in San Carlos to have released on bail till their hearing.

"I never heard of that being done by telegraph," Raider said. "I thought there had to be a preliminary hearing before a judge. You sure this is legal?"

The sheriff shrugged. "What I'm sure of is that this is West Texas and Noah Blake's got some mighty powerful friends. My deputies are freeing those men right now, giving them back their guns. I thought you and Weatherbee might like to know about it.''

"I appreciate you telling me.''

The sheriff left the saloon, and Raider didn't think too much more about it. He wasn't even surprised when he saw all seven walk into the Horseshoe and celebrate at the bar. They pretended not to see him, but Raider knew right well that they knew he was there. And without Doc. Raider expected trouble, but he just wasn't the kind to go scampering across the road to the hotel looking for his partner's help. When the day came that he couldn't look after himself by himself, he'd stay home—wherever that was.

He watched for them to break up into twos and threes or for some of them to maybe drift around to tables behind him, spread out, close in on him—but they did none of that. Linda Sue and he chatted on, sipping at the good bourbon, while Raider tried to convince her that by getting him instead of Doc she had got the better bargain—she didn't seem too convinced so far by what he was saying. As he talked, his mind focused on his present danger.

Four of them were regular cowhands on Blake's spread, probably not too fast or too free with a gun, leastways not professionals. Three were so-called bounty hunters—maybe just drifters in search of an easy buck. None of them had the cold, calculating eyes of the real professional, the loner who survives because he tips the odds in his favor. These were just roughnecks who got by through picking on the weak. And no doubt at odds of seven to one, that's what they considered him to be right now.

"Let me hold your shawl for you," Raider offered, taking it from the back of the empty chair next to Linda Sue.

"No, it's all right where it was—" Linda Sue stopped as she saw him drape the shawl loosely over his right hand. She was young, but not inexperienced in the ways of saloon life. "You burn any holes in that shawl, it'll cost you five dollars."

"Why don't you go over and stand by the window," he told her. "Nod to me if you see Doc coming back."

She didn't need any second urging to move out of the way of future gunplay.

Raider sat at the table and waited, almost directly facing the backs of the seven men grouped together at the bar. He smiled to himself knowingly as he saw them become increasingly quiet. They all put their glasses on the counter. One of the four cowhands could not help glancing nervously over his shoulder at him. One of the three gunmen, still facing the bar, went for his revolver.

The silk shawl over Raider's right hand jumped as the bullet swept out of its folds and hit the gunman in the side before he could fully turn around. The .44 bullet punched a hole the size and shape of a hen's egg in the side of the man's yellow shirt, and the gun fell from his hand as his knees buckled.

Raider noticed none of this. He had thumbed back the hammer and squeezed off a second shot, which blew away the silk shawl, uncovering his smoking gun, and hit the second gunman in the bridge of his nose. He was thrown back against the bar counter and slid gently into a sitting position on the floor, the middle of his face drilled as if the tip of a horn had gored it.

The third gunman let his Colt Peacemaker slide back into its holster and moved his right hand away from its handle, very deliberately, so as there would be no misunderstanding.

None of the four cowmen had even managed to clear the barrel of their guns from leather, and already two of their friends were dead on the floor, killed by a single man! They had no chance here. Now they knew it.

Which was the moment Doc chose to walk in, with Adele on his arm. He looked relaxed, bathed, loved, and impeccably dressed. Doc smoothed his cravat and looked first at the two dead men and then at Raider, as a sorrowing parent might at a naughty boy.

"Been at it again, Raider." He turned to the five miserable survivors. "You should have stayed in jail. You'd have been safer there."

CHAPTER TEN

The almost full moon gave the five men light to ride back
that night to the bunkhouses of the Tumbling K. As they
got onto the spread, the sound of their horses disturbed a
herd of longhorn steers grazing nearby.

"You going to be staying around?" one of the cowhands asked the sole surviving gunman.

"You think I'm loco? Not with those damn Pinkertons."

"You going to let them scare you off, just like that?"
another cowboy taunted.

"You bet I am," the gunman answered without anger.
"If you had any brains, you'd clear out too. You going to
wait around for them to put you on trial and maybe hang
you?"

The four cowhands were silent at this.

"What do you boys make in a month anyhow?" the
gunman went on. "Twenty dollars?"

"Mr. Blake pays a dollar a day to an experienced
man," one of the cowhands boasted.

"With your kind of skill in handling cattle, you could make ten a day rustling," the gunman retorted. "And that's without straining yourself or taking much risk. And I sure don't mean stealing stupid bawling calves from their mothers on the big boss's instructions so he can break some squatter on a stream bank. I mean real rustling. Look at that herd yonder. Imagine what the five of us could make on those beasts . . . if you had any guts and weren't sticking on here in order to get hung."

One of the cowboys laughed a mite too loudly. "Where would you take them with that brand? Up to Kansas?"

"We'd never get away with that—not with a well-known brand like that and so many cattle," the gunman explained. "You know that as well as I do. What we'd have to do is drive them without stopping south of the border and sell them for next to nothing, payment in gold and no questions asked. How many head do you reckon there are?"

"More than four hundred."

The gunman figured it out in his mind. "You can depend on five dollars a head at the least. Which comes to two thousand for four hundred head. Splitting that five ways gives each man four hundred dollars for a couple of days' work. As I said, we get paid in gold." He reined his horse to a very slow walk. "If you want to do it, we'd need to get them on the move now. . . ."

The gunman knew enough to shut up and let them come to their own decision. They had also slowed their horses to a walk, and each man now rode in the moonlight with his own thoughts and emotions. They said nothing to each other, just simply walked slowly along, maybe hoping the stars would tell them what to do.

One cowhand pulled his horse to a halt. The man near-

est him went on a few paces before he turned his horse
completely around. The other two wheeled their horses
about, with wild grins on their faces.

"Yahoo!" one yelled, slapping his horse's flank with
his hat. "Let's move that beef down south and get our
hands on some señoritas!"

While Blake's four cowhands and the gunman were
driving off one of the Tumbling K herds by moonlight, El
Caballito del Diablo was running in a crouch from shadow
to shadow by the bunkhouses. He carried bulging armfuls
of withered dry brush in several journeys to the cabin where
Mournful John McClintock slept. After he had piled up a
sizeable stack of the brush, he placed it in small bundles
against the base of the cabin's wooden walls. Then, moving without a sound, he lit each of the bundles of dry brush
so that they sprang up in yellow flames with a loud
crackling noise.

The sharp points of the flames licked up along all four
cabin walls, with an extra-large fuel supply stacked up
against the outside of the door. Caballito found the smell
of wood smoke pleasant in his nostrils. He backed away
out of the flickering light cast by the flames, and eased
himself out of the moonlight into a long shadow by a
corral, where he waited hunkered down with his rifle
across his knees.

As the flames grew high against the walls of the cabin,
the horses in the corral began to neigh and gallop back and
forth in panic. The animals weren't threatened, but their
instinctive dread of fire caused them to become increasingly
agitated and to whinny and bang against the corral rails in
their efforts to escape.

Caballito saw the cabin door open, saw a face for a

moment in the glow of the flames, and then the figure
retreated inside as the burning sticks piled against the door
fell inward. Smoke billowed out the doorway. Mournful
John would soon be forced out—or else he would be
overcome by smoke and burned to a cinder. Flames had
caught the front of the roof now, and soon flaming bits
would be dropping down into the interior of the cabin.
Caballito levered a shell into posiion in his rifle. He waited
calmly in the long shadow.

The figure appeared inside the doorway again and, with
a forearm raised before his face, rushed through the barrier
of flames into the open. The back of the man's shirt was
afire. Before Caballito could get a shot at him, cowhands
raised by the noise of the horses or by the crackling and
the light of the fire itself were rolling him on the ground to
extinguish the flames on his burning clothes. He distinctly
heard one man say, "Mr. McClintock." Caballito nosed
among them with the sights of his rifle barrel, looking for
a clear shot among them in the moonlight at Mournful
John. It was a pity to have to shoot him—much better to
have burned him to death.

Caballito found it hard to see the foremost sight by
moonlight, but nevertheless was ready when McClintock
sat up and had a clear line of fire. He missed! He knew he
had as soon as he squeezed the trigger. Caballito jerked
another shell into the firing chamber and got off a quick
second shot at his target. He missed again.

They were firing back at him. His two rifle flashes had
given them a good idea of his position, and they were
peppering the whole area with lead. With a sudden dart, he
made his way across open ground to the cover of the
bunkhouse. They saw him go, but he had been too quick
for them to fire upon him. From this position, he now

could drive them behind the burning cabin for cover if he chose. But once again Caballito was looking for just one man. As he searched for a shot at Mournful John from the cover of the bunkhouse, someone inside lit an oil lamp and turned it on full. Caballito found himself illuminated from a window next to his head.

He heard the cries of the men at the cabin, "It's that Injun! El Caballito del Diablo! The Comanche renegade that's with them Pinkertons!"

A bullet flew past his nose. Another touched the skin on the back of his left hand. Someone inside the bunkhouse was shooting out at him through the wooden wall. Another bullet whistled past him, and another exit hole appeared in the wood next to his face. Caballito ran.

He made a good distance across the clear ground by moonlight before his adversaries realized he was on the run. Then they had to cover the yardage from the cabin to the bunkhouse and themselves enter open ground without protection from there on. They knew better than that.

Caballito was almost to where he had tethered his horse in a thicket when he heard hoofbeats behind him. He turned and got down on one knee. Three riders were coming after him, hoping to run him down on the open ground. He raised his rifle and aimed for the lead rider but apparently hit the horse in the head, because it collapsed in a spinning heap and threw its rider on the ground.

The others turned their mounts around, and the fallen man vaulted on behind one of them as they rode back to the corral. At that moment Caballito realized that the lead horseman in all likelihood had been Mournful John. Had either of the other two been McClintock, he wouldn't have given up the hunt so easily, and it was unlikely that he would have let three others do his dirty work for him.

For a moment Caballito sighted along the rifle barrel at this man's back, but then his finger loosened on the trigger. Backshooting was not the Comanche way of dealing with an enemy.

It occurred to the lieutenant as he rode into Williamville that a lot of people hereabouts did not seem to care for the sight of a Union army uniform. Even though it appeared to be fresh in the minds of some, that trouble was long past—neither Lieutenant Green nor any of his men had been old enough to fight in that war. Yet the blue uniforms seemed to touch many raw wounds and exposed nerves.

This was not Lieutenant Abel Green's only trouble. He and his nineteen men had been selected as a so-called expeditionary force along the border with Mexico. They had been out in the field almost a month now and had another two weeks ahead of them. An ambitious young officer could use such an opportunity to engage the little army that was temporarily his to rule in some kind of conflict, emerge victorious, and return to write a glowing report on his deeds and achievements. There was not much other hope for quick advancement in peacetime. When there was no war for a forceful officer to shine in, he could excel in a skirmish of his own making. Green's expedition had been disastrous. The men had got drunk and fought with the locals in almost every town they had come to. He had lost one soldier and had four dead civilians to account for in three towns. His sergeant had been lavish with their funds, so that now they would have to live on beans and bread for the next two weeks. The ranks were sulking listlessly and penniless outside in the street while the lieutenant and sergeant allowed themselves conference costs in the Horseshoe Saloon.

"I know you're the one who takes the credit or the blame," the sergeant conceded without seeming to care one way or the other.

He was a stocky, dissolute-looking man. His hair was thinning on top, and his eyes had heavy lids that readily drooped. The lieutenant was thin, nervous, and voluble. His hands were long and bony, and lay as motionless as two small dead animals on the table before him.

"The blame—no one's talking about credit," the officer informed the sergeant. "What we need now is some kind of minor Alamo."

"With you the sole survivor," the sergeant added grimly.

"Of course. But your memory would live ever green in my mind and heart, Sergeant."

"You gotta think of something."

The lieutenant noticed that the sergeant had given up calling him "sir" except opposite the men. "Well, the Mexican army is south of the border where it belongs, Quantrill's Raiders if they were still around would kick the shit out of us, the Indians in these parts have all been removed to the Indian Territory—"

"I can get you Indians."

The two soldiers looked at the man who had made this statement, obviously after eavesdropping on their conversation. He was a prosperous-looking individual, alone at a table with a bottle of fine bourbon. When he gestured to chairs on either side of him, they did not hesitate.

"My name is Noah Blake," the man went on. "I've a big spread outside town, and last night I lost a herd of four hundred steers to a band of renegade Comanches led by one who calls himself El Cabillito del Diablo. There's a bunkhouse at my place for you men, with free food while they're helping to root out this Indian menace. So far as I am concerned, you, Lieutenant, will get complete and sole credit for everything we achieve together.'' He poured them each a generous measure of the amber fluid. ''And of course, Lieutenant, you will stay in my home as a guest of my family. General Bridges, by the way, is an old friend of mine. . . .''

Doc, Raider, and Caballito had spent a fruitless morning riding the range. They had set out shortly after daybreak and were returning to the Dunwell ranch house at close to noon in order to escape the hottest hour of the day.

''Raider and I are totally recovered now from those gunshot wounds,'' Doc was saying as they rode three abreast toward the house. ''If Wagner in the Chicago office would see us spending our days in this leisurely way, I think he'd find some suicide detail for us in an hour flat. We've had only four telegrams—all wishing us a speedy recovery and telling us to take it easy.''

''Doc's afraid they're about to retire us to desk jobs,'' Raider said.

Caballito laughed. ''I will tell you what I think. In that office they know that you two will not stay quietly in one place for long if you can help it, so since you are still here, they have to think that both of you are still sick. Since they don't know about Mournful John.''

''They don't,'' Doc confirmed.

''Maybe you two should go away,'' Caballito suggested. ''There's much Pinkerton work to be done. Most of the bounty hunters have already gone, since they've seen there are no easy pickings. The rest will go now, since Raider killed those two in Williamville. Leave Mournful John McClintock to me. A homeless Comanche warrior has nothing else to do with his days but hunt down his enemies and settle old scores. I will make him pay for what he did to you two as well as to my friend Crazy Joe Fields."

"To tell the truth, Caballito," Doc said, "if this only came down to waiting about to get a crack at Mournful John, I'd say to hell with it and move on. Vengeance carried too far sours a man. There's no righteousness in it after a while, only viciousness."

The Comanche smiled grimly. "The white man likes to reason everything away."

"Not quite everything," Doc objected. "So long as Blake keeps Mournful John in his hire, along with those two Harris brothers they spared from hanging, we got a problem here."

"Damn right," Raider put in.

"So we're not quite ready yet to hand over Mournful John to you alone," Doc said. "In my opinion, I'll get him before either of you."

Caballito laughed. "Your mind is leading you astray again." He tapped the side of his skull. "Too much sun."

"All Northerners get like that down here," Raider agreed.

"There's a strange horse in that corral," Caballito observed.

How he noticed one horse among the thirty or so in that corral was beyond Raider and Doc. They went through their almost automatic precautions on approaching the building, splitting up, covering each other. Sarah Cooper sat at the kitchen table, talking with Will Tucker. She ignored Doc and ran up to Raider and kissed him on the cheek.

Raider grinned and wasn't fooled. She wasn't the first woman to try to get back at Doc by using him.

Doc as always seemed to be unaware of a woman's ploys and went his own relaxed, casual way. Sarah wearied of her game when she saw Raider wouldn't go along with it and Doc didn't care.

"I heard all about you and that blond hussy in Williamville," she burst out angrily.

"Adele?" Doc queried.

"That bitch! That whore—"

"Now, now," Doc calmed her. "It's true that Adele lacks many of your personal qualities, Sarah, but you mustn't be too hard on her."

There were other men present, and Sarah had been brought up to behave in a certain way opposite men, so that she found herself unable to give vent to the anger she felt, to allow her feelings to escape freely in whatever words happened to fit them, no matter how unladylike. When she and Doc were alone, she would let him know exactly how she felt. Meanwhile there were important things to do. Sarah Cooper was a governess, and above all a practical and disciplined woman.

"I didn't come here to discuss some slut in the town," she said with dignity. "I came here to tell you that Mr. Blake is presently entertaining a Lieutenant Abel Green in his house and has nineteen soldiers billeted in the bunkhouses. At dinner last night the lieutenant was quite excited about catching the Comanche renegades Mr. Blake has been telling him about. He thinks there are quite a lot of them and that they are led by El Caballito del Diablo."

"Soldiers . . ." Caballito's voice was almost inaudible, but they were startled by the ferocity of its tone.

Doc asked, "Did Blake say anything to him about Pinkerton agents?"

"No, but I did," Sarah replied. "The lieutenant showed no interest in any complications like that. He didn't want to hear what I had to say and asked me to play the piano instead. He wants to believe there's a bunch of wild Indians out there against which he can lead a cavalry charge.''

Caballito sat silently, smoldering.

''Thanks for coming to tell us,'' Raider said. ''Someone who held a grudge might not have come.''

''That's true,'' Doc said contritely and squeezed her hand. ''Blake must know you came.''

''I know for certain that he wanted me to come,'' Sarah said, ''by the way he steered the lieutenant's talk. Normally he never allows such conversation at the dinner table. I think he wants to frighten Caballito away.''

The Comanche rose to his feet. ''I will return,'' he said and left.

In a few minutes they heard his horse galloping away.

''The Injun was seen riding for the hills,'' Ned Harris told his brother Jake and Mournful John McClintock.

Jake's bullet head nodded happily. He turned his good eye toward Mournful John and said, ''Ranch hands farther west saw him.''

''Just like that,'' Mournful John said doubtfully.

''Injuns do that,'' Ned explained. ''They don't stand their ground like us and fight till the last man. When things go agin them, they turn tail and run.''

''But turn around and fight you again when you least expect it,'' Mournful John added dourly.

There was no denying this, and the Harris brothers kept silent.

The three men rode side by side westward from the Tumbling K ranch house. The Harris brothers were watchful, knowing that McClintock had something on his mind. They wondered what it was. After a time of riding without saying anything, McClintock spoke again. He was still going on about that Indian.

"For whatever reason, leastways he's gone for a while. I don't think this is the last we'll see of him, so we should take advantage of things while he's gone."

They rode on some more in melancholy silence while the Harrises played a game of wait and see. They were afraid of Mournful John. Even out on the range, two against one. They owed him, for not hanging them. And they owed Blake three hundred dollars each for the bounty he had paid on them as rustlers. Mournful John was holding them to that debt, and he was crazy enough to chase them to the Pacific if they ran out on him. The brothers had discussed all this endlessly and had reached a joint conclusion: Wait and see.

"While that Comanche is gone," Mournful John went on in his ponderous way, "is the time to rid ourselves of those two others."

Ned's dead eyes looked out above his sunken cheeks and gaunt frame. "It don't pay to kill Pinkertons."

"What have you got to lose?" Mournful John asked. "If the Pinkertons come after anyone, it will be me, not you, and I ain't worried."

"I don't like it," Ned said. "I mean I'd be happy to kill 'em both to oblige a friend like you, John, but it's what comes after that bothers me."

Mournful John sneered. "Since when did worrying about the consequences ever stop either of you from doing what you wanted?"

The Harrises had to laugh at that. It was not often that McClintock make a joke.

"You'd be free of your obligation to me and to Noah Blake—don't matter which of us kills who," McClintock offered. "Just ride with me and take them on. After they're dead, we'll all be even."

Jake exposed his five remaining teeth in a grin. "That sounds right tempting to me, John."

His brother Ned was more reluctant. "I can see your point of us hitting them while the Injun is away. That makes sense. I just think there must be some other way of dealing with them besides killing them."

"When you think of it, let me know," Mournful John said sarcastically. "With any other man but you, Ned, I might think he was afeared of them two Pinkertons."

Ned was too old a hand to rise to that bait. "Oh, I got respect for them, I tell you. Like I would for a grizzly or a rattler. But I ain't afeared of them."

They rode on a piece more in silence, all the time heading for the ridge beyond which lay the Dunwell property.

"What have you got in mind, John?" Ned finally asked.

McClintock answered readily enough, "There's a gulch with steep sides in those big hills on the far side of the Dunwell ranch. The gulch is wide as you enter it, but when you follow it along it goes into a bottleneck. It ain't a box canyon, because there's a way out at its head by the dried-up creek bed. So if the Pinkertons do know it, they won't feel they're being led into a dead-end trap. But one man with a rifle could block off the head. So if I was to lead them in and you two was to follow after, there's a mighty good chance we could collect the hides of a couple of varmints that've been bothering us."

Raider and Doc saw Will Tucker galloping like grazy toward them. His horse's hooves kicked up a lingering cloud of gray dust behind him.

"It's McClintock!" Will yelled while he was still fifty yards away. "I've just seen him!"

His horse twisted and reared its forelegs in the air.

"Not twenty minutes ago he passed by himself just north of the house. I could hardly believe my eyes. Well out of rifle range, mind you, but there he was, in broad daylight, Mournful John McClintock riding due west across this ranch after putting its owner in the grave. I know it's a trap of some kind, so I didn't go after him myself."

"You did right," Doc said. "We'll drop you off at the ranch house and you keep your eyes peeled there—in case he's trying to lure us away from the house so the Harris brothers can burn it down."

"There's a ranch hand there now, and I know this is a trap," Will warned them again.

Raider grinned. "There's nothing I like better than riding into a trap."

Doc sighed. "He means it."

After leaving Will at the ranch house, they rode at a canter in the direction Mournful John had taken. After half an hour they saw a lone figure moving slowly ahead. The rider looked back over his shoulder, saw them, and quickened his pace. They couldn't be sure yet that it was McClintock, but it looked reasonably like him. Tucker had been sure.

"The bastard is making for that gulch through the hills," Raider said. "We got to cut him off before he gets to it or else follow him in. Be a good place to be bushwhacked."

"I remember the place," Doc said.

They spurred their horses, but as they galloped after the mounted man, he also speeded up his horse and maintained the distance between them. As they neared the big hills, all three riders were galloping flat out until Doc and

Raider eased their pace on seeing they could not cut him off before he reached the gulch. Now they had to make up their minds whether to risk following him in. Or at least Doc had to. Raider had his mind already made up. He was going in.

The creek bed at the bottom of the gulch was almost dry, hardly more than a trickle from one large stagnant puddle to the next among the loose rounded boulders. The sloping sides consisted of reddish shale that easily shattered and flaked away beneath their horses' hooves. There was no growth, no cover for bushwhackers. No sign of riders on the range behind them. The gulch was empty except for the rider ahead of them, whose horse was picking its way on the crumbling shale alongside the rocks in the creek bottom.

"The gulch narrows at the far end," Raider said. "That has to be where he'll try to hit us."

"If we let him. I think we can climb up along the sides above him."

"Unless he's already thought of that," Raider said. "Let's find out."

Like so many of their other discussions on what to do, this talk was conducted on the move. Doc and Raider didn't go in much for hesitation.

They had explored this gulch once before, and Doc tried to recall what lay on the other side, while looking anxiously at the makings of a mountain storm brewing to the northwest of them.

"We break out on a high grassland plateau at the end of the gulch," Doc remembered. "But if we get a storm in these hills, we're going to lose him in the rain. We won't have a chance of catching him."

Raider nodded and glanced up at the tumbling black and

gray clouds, which seemed to mix and roll like quicksilver down from the high peaks beyond the hills they were in.

"I ain't turning back," he muttered in a way which Doc understood to mean that turning back would have been his advice to anyone else but himself.

In another minute they discovered they couldn't turn back even if they wanted to. A bullet whistled over Raider's right shoulder and dug in a pockmark in the red shale a few yards off. A second—this one aimed at Doc—richocheted among a dozen smooth boulders in the dry stream bed. Two horsemen had ridden into the gulch behind them and were firing on their backs with rifles. This was a signal to the rider in front, presumably McClintock, to turn around. His bullet cut up a spurt of red powder from the shale between their two horses.

"Damn, those two behind had to be in hiding in the hills till they saw us come in here," Raider growled.

"I think Will Tucker mentioned it might be a trap," Doc said drily.

And they saw what a hell of a trap it was. Their three attackers didn't have to move in close for an accurate shot. They could rely on the slow going underfoot—either on the rocky bottom or on the crumbling sides of the gulch—to slow the Pinkertons' horses sufficiently to provide lots of time for picking them off.

Doc and Raider didn't dare stand still and present themselves as immobile targets in order to return fire properly. The largest boulders on the stream bottom were the size of melons—nothing behind which they could take cover unless they built a dry-stone wall of them, and the three riflemen were sure going to prevent that!

The Pinkertons looked at the sky again, this time hopefully. If anything was going to save them now, it was heavy rain. Rain had already obscurred the peaks from view off to the northwest, but these mountain storms were often local—this one might deluge a place a mile away without their getting a drop of rain.

They kept on the move one slope of the gulch, weaving in and out, and fired back from the hip with their rifles at the three horsemen, levering shells quickly and keeping up a steady rapid fire which made it more difficult for their attackers to take calm and steady aim. They eased up only to reload—and finally when they heard a great roar approaching them fast.

Raider looked startled. "I didn't know there was a railroad here."

"Sure sounds like a train," Doc said, "but we'd have seen the rails before now or heard about it."

His voice was cut off by the deafening roar, louder now than that of the fastest locomotive, literally shaking the earth beneath their horses' hooves.

All thought of combat was forgotten as the five horsemen in the gulch looked toward the source of the enormous sound at the neck of the gulch. A brown head of water, like that of a big serpent, darted into the gulch along the dry creek bed. The wall of water rushed in from the mountain peaks, bearing rocks, pieces of tree trunks, and gravel and soil—picking up whatever lay in its path and bearing it along. In seconds the creek bed at the head of the gulch and its dry sunbaked rocks and stagnant puddles had disappeared in the brown, swirling flood which had climbed up to the belly of McClintock's horse.

Then a surge of brown water lifted the horse off its feet, knocking the rider from the saddle. Both man and animal could only struggle to keep their heads above the rushing brown flood as they were swept downstream.

Doc and Raider urged their horses higher up the slope. What had once been the dry bottom beneath them was now ten feet deep in the gurgling flood, and they could hear the heavy knocking sound of boulders bouncing along the bottom.

As the gulch widened, the force of the water was dissipated and its depth lessened. Doc and Raider managed to stay above its rising tide. As the rider and horse were borne past them in the flood, Raider raised his carbine.

"It's McClintock," he ground out and sighted along the barrel.

Doc said nothing as he watched him follow the bobbing head in the sights. He smiled as Raider put down the carbine without having fired a shot.

"Nothing wrong with being tempted to shoot him while he's helpless," Raider muttered. "But it'll be more fun to watch him drown."

Mournful John McClintock did not drown. The rise of the water level was only three or four feet farther down the gulch, and the Harris brothers forced their horses out into the current and pulled McClintock out of the water. His horse found its own footing and clambered after them.

Doc lit an old Virginia cheroot. "So we all live to fight another day."

CHAPTER ELEVEN

Doc and Raider's first run-in with Lieutenant Abel Green and his men hadn't gone too well. The action-hungry lieutenant had tried to present himself as the voice of government to the two Pinkertons, and they had laughed at him.

"Sit yourself down and have a cup of coffee," Raider told him. "We don't understand any of your Washington talk, and neither will any of these Indians you're going on about."

"I'm going to find them," the lieutenant said grimly.

"If they're here at all," Raider assured him, "they'll find you first and you'll know all about it."

"It's my government-appointed duty and sacred honor to disarm these savages and return them to their reservations," the lieutenant intoned. "Any man who stands between me and the carrying out of my duty is a traitor of the United States."

Raider guffawed. "If there was a bunch of wild Indians

with guns around here, like you say there is, any man who stood between you and them would be crazy as well as a traitor.''

"I certainly wouldn't risk it," Doc said very gravely.

The lieutenant knew he was being put on and resented it. "I've had information that a Comanche renegade name El Caballito del Diablo is an associate of yours.''

"Yes, he is," Doc confirmed.

"He's a wanted man," Lieutenant Green said.

"We're Pinkerton agents, not Texas law-enforcement officers," Doc said. "We'd be out of line in interfering in anything without being directed to do so by our office.''

"Caballito is the leader of this Indian band," the lieutenant said.

"He's a loner," Raider insisted.

Then the lieutenant began again on the powers invested in him by Washington, and Doc and Raider began making fun of him again.

They ran into the lieutenant or patrols of his men at all hours.

"These soldiers are good for you small ranchers," Doc told Will Tucker. "Blake and McClintock or other big landowners can't make trouble for you while they're around as witnesses. I think Blake's lash has curled back on himself.''

"Better relax while the soldiers are still around," Raider advised. "They'll get weary soon enough looking for these imaginary Indians and move on.''

"Where the hell is Caballito?" Tucker asked.

"Damned if I know," Raider answered. "It'd be nice if he stayed away till these Yankee troops move out.''

Thus it was with consternation that Doc and Raider

listened the next day to what Will Tucker said he had seen an hour previously.

"I'd swear most of 'em were Apaches," Tucker went on emotionally. "Small and stocky, dark skins, long hair, headband knotted on the side with the loose ends hanging down. You ever seen Apaches?"

Doc and Raider nodded.

"You find them west of here in New Mexico and southwest across the border in Old Mexico," Tucker said. "Some of the others were Comanches—at least they looked real close to Caballito himself. He was riding as their leader and ignored me. All of them just rode past me like I didn't exist. Like they were ghosts. Except that I got the strangest feeling that they were the ones who were real and I was the ghost."

"They sound real flesh and blood all right," Doc said. "I only wish you were imagining things."

"But the Comanches and Apaches never got along well together," Tucker said.

"Maybe having one last crack at the U.S. Army was enough to settle their differences," Doc said. "You say they just rode past you, heading north along the stream? They could be headed anywhere. How many of them were there?"

"Fifteen, sixteen."

"I'm wondering what we should do," Doc said. "That lieutenant will never believe us now that these Indians weren't here till he set out to look for them."

"I know what I'm going to do about it," Raider said, looking immensely pleased. "Take an afternoon nap on it."

•   •   •

"We've sighted them, sir!" the lookouts yelled as they galloped toward hte Tumbling K corrals. "Apaches and Comanches! We counted sixteen of them!"

Lieutenant Green gave word to the sergeant, who ordered weapons and ammunition distributed, horses saddled, and every man present.

Mournful John McClintock glanced across at Noah Blake as they heard the news and saw the soldiers' preparations under way.

"I think maybe it's some of them young sons of the small ranchers playing tricks," Mournful John opined.

Noah Blake was more doubtful. He had become irritated by McClintock's dour manner and by the man's open lack of concern with what happened to anyone save himself. Blake was beginning to find the soldiers' presence a burden also, and he realized it would be simple for Caballito to outwait the soldiers and, after they had gone, return with renewed vengeance. Blake of course did not know that the Comanche was interested only in killing Mournful John—the landowner had always assumed that he and his property were Caballito's targets. This was not an unreasonable assumption, since all of Blake's huge spread had been Comanche land not very long ago.

"I don't like the sound of this," Blake said to McClintock. "Those soldiers had already become suspicious of the tall tales we told them of Indian marauders. They spoke to other people out on the ranges and were laughed at. Now, all of a sudden, they believe—after Caballito has been gone for days. I just hope we haven't brought something even worse than rustlers upon our heads."

Mournful John dismissed these fanciful worries with a snicker. Blake was fool. These soldiers were fools. Apaches!

Comanches! Next they would be talking about drums and war dances and hiding their women and children!

Old Andrew Allen had always expected that the Comanches would come back. His son, who ran his huge ranch now while the old man sat in the shade, had been only a small boy when old Andrew used to have frequent running battles with Comanche warriors as he tended his cattle. His grandsons, now about the same age as their father had been then, had never even seen an Indian—let alone a Comanche warrior prepared for combat. They didn't know what he was talking about. Old Andrew was well aware that his grandsons thought their grandpa a little bit loco, with all his strange talk and his keeping a wary eye on the horizon and a loaded rifle never too far out of reach. Times have changed, Grandpa, they were always telling him. However, he knew that some day the Comanches would come back.

"Injuns!" Grandpa Allen yelled and reached for his Remington rifle beside him on the porch. "Injuns!"

Inside the house, his son winked at his own sons and told them, "Go out and help Grandpa fight the Comanches."

They heard the old man's rifle fire out on the porch and the boys' mother called to them, "Stay inside! That crazy old bird is likely to think it's you who's attacking him."

The boys' father laughed good-naturedly and, as the shots continued outside on the porch, went to investigate what his own father's doting imagination had produced. He hoped the old man's rifle hadn't hit any of the horses in the corral.

The scene that met his eyes was like an episode from one of old Andrew's more unbelievable stories. A group of mounted soldiers were galloping across the range to the sanctuary of the ranch house with a band of Indians hot in pursuit. They were still so far away that the shots they were firing at each other could hardly be heard. All were well out of range of the old man's Remington, which he had fired till empty and was now reloading.

Andrew Jr. Ran back inside the house. "Get in the root cellar! Your Grandpa is right! Hide! Hide!"

He grabbed a rifle and stuffed his pockets with shells. Then he escorted his wife and three children, with a large pitcher of drinking water and two loaves of bread, to the root cellar in back of the ranch house. When they were inside, he lowered the door and scattered grass stalks as best he could to conceal the entrance. He supposed grimly that this would not be enough to fool Indians—and for a moment he wished he recalled more useful details of the old man's stories.

"Quiet down!" he shouted to his wife and children. "I can hear your voices from here. Whatever happens, don't make a sound till they've been gone for hours."

This was met by sobbing and calls for "Daddy, Daddy," as they realized they might never see him alive again.

"Hush now!"

He ran to join old Andrew on the porch, changed his mind, and rushed to open the gate of the corral nearest the house so the soldiers could loose their horses within it and make for the house with the least loss of time.

Both horses and soldiers were covered in sweat and dust. The soldiers dragged their rifles indoors and knocked out the glass from windows to take aim at the approaching Indians. But these wheeled away before coming into rifle range. Only old Andrew, with his defective sight, kept blasting away at them.

A long wait followed. A few Indians constantly circled the house well out of range in order to raise the alarm if anyone tried to escape. The others butchered two steers, made a huge fire from the rails of a far corral, and prepared a feast. After sunset the men in the ranch house could see them eating and resting. In the darkness the flames died down, and they could see nothing. They debated whether a small group should creep away in the dark to fetch help. But they decided to stay put and fight off the siege.

They kept their weary eyes open, searching the darkness for a movement or the hint of a sneak attack. Their eyes and ears played tricks on them. They fired occasionally at what proved to be empty space. Or had it been? They listened. Just before dawn they heard a jackrabbit screaming, caught in the jaws of a coyote or a bobcat. Old Andrew swore it wasn't a real jackrabbit but a Comanche signal to attack. They waited, tensed. Yet nothing happened. Daylight came before they realized the Indians had gone.

Two days after the "incident" at the Allen ranch, Will Tucker arrived at the Dunwell ranch house in great humor and demanded that Doc and Raider sit with him to hear his good news.

"Me and some of the other small ranchers went to this meeting held at the Allen ranch. The Allens weren't as bad as some of the big landowners, but when Blake's dirty work was to their advantage, you didn't hear them complaining and talking about justice. Their ranch house was a shambles. They were still mad as hell and blamed Blake for everything, now that things have gone wrong for them."

"What did they want with you?" Doc asked.

"To make peace."

"On what terms?"

Will Tucker laughed and wagged his forefinger in Doc's face. "You think us small ranchers couldn't manage on our own? That we shouldn't have gone without you two? Well, here's the terms. They break up their association and we break up ours, that we all become neighbors once again and respect each other's property and boundaries. That the bounty on rustlers and other lures for gunmen and drifters be stopped right away. And, listen to this, that they pay your Pinkerton fees and continue to do so at full rate as long as you're needed in these parts."

"Not bad at all," Raider complimented him. "Was Noah Blake present?"

"Certainly," Tucker said. "He walked out without a word at the end. And one more thing. They want you to do something."

"What's that?" Doc asked suspiciously.

"Ask Caballito to send his friends back where they came from."

El Caballito del Diablo rode at the head of the band in the first gray light of dawn across the southernmost reaches of the Tumbling K spread. The Apaches in particular were distrustful of Caballito's motives, especially since he said he was not going along with them.

"What about the lieutenant and the soldiers?" one Apache asked him.

"Half of them went into town last night and celebrated on money they got somehow," Caballito said. "Most of them are probably still in Williamville. It'll be five or six hours before the lieutenant can organize his men."

"I didn't come here to steal," another Apache claimed. "I came to fight soldiers."

"You can always let them catch up with you if that's what you want," Caballito said. "The *brasada* south of here will make a better place to fight them than the open land around here."

"True," the Apache agreed.

The group rode on across the Tumbling K, two hours' ride below the Blake ranch house.

"You'll have a day's start on the soldiers before they can follow you," Caballito summed it up. "I think you should lose them and keep going."

They said nothing. Caballito knew they were disappointed in only one skirmish with the soldiers. There had been no clashes since the single chase across the Allen ranch. Now the Indians were getting boastful and overconfident. The lieutenant and his men might have a nasty surprise in store for them yet. In another way, Caballito was sorry to see them go. It had been good to ride with his people—and even their traditional enemies, the Apaches—to ride over their ancestral lands and drive their enemies before them like frightened deer.

Caballito would return to his solitary life among the hills. He had no desire to join a raiding band like this one, skipping back and forth across the border, always on the move. Such a life of parasitizing the white invader was not independence. He could only find that alone in the hills. After he had disposed of his enemy. After he had honored the spirit of Crazy Joe Fields by spilling the blood of Mournful John McClintock.

They followed the course of a dried-up stream bed and passed around the base of a rocky bluff that stood alone on the level rangeland. Once they rounded the bluff, Caballito did not need to point. An enormous herd of longhorns grazed quietly before them.

"How many?" one of the Comanches asked in an impressed voice.

"Yesterday I reckoned on close to eighteen hundred head," Caballito said.

"We take them all?" the Comanche asked.

Caballito smiled. "I don't need any."

They bade him farewell quietly so as not to spook the grazing herd. They were well satisfied now and had already forgotten their wish for more fighting with the soldiers. Caballito watched as they expertly circled around behind the herd and began to urge it forward at a walking pace, turning back strays on the flanks, yet keeping away so the cattle could set their own pace and avoid a stampede. The huge herd began to move across the land southward, thick as a swarm of honeybees.

Noah Blake was distraught. "I'm ruined!" he bellowed. "I've lost more than two thousand head of cattle since you've set foot on this ranch, McClintock. Rustlers used to take fifty or sixty at a time. Instead of helping, you've made things worse!"

McClintock's expression grew more dour than usual. He said nothing.

Blake ignored his dangerous silence and ranted on. "I would have been better off allowing myself to be robbed on a samll scale. My losses would have been reasonable. I could have afforded them. Two thousand head of cattle! More than that! First, some of your no-good bounty hunters persuaded my own ranch hands to drive off four hundred head. Then these Indians grab at least eighteen hundred more. Green and his troops didn't leave till early this morning, and if those cattle were stolen yesterday at dawn or earlier, they've built up a hell of a lead on him. You refuse to do anything. I can't understand that. Are you afraid of Apaches and Comanches? You and the Harrises could have caught up with them and killed some of them. I'd have paid you. I still will. Three hundred dollars per man you kill. I don't care what those fool landowners say. I don't want peace. I want blood! I've been robbed! Are you listening?''

McClintock nodded dolefully.

"People can't do this to me! I'm Noah Blake! You hear? Damnit, man, say something!''

McClintock said nothing.

"I'm a ruined man," Blake fumed. "Ruined! More than two thousand head of livestock gone. And I don't expect that fool sheriff and his deputies will find anything. I'd follow the thieves myself if I thought I could leave here, but I tremble to think what worse could befall my family in my absence. I—''

Just as Noah Blake was getting himself whipped up into another burst of rage, Jake Harris interrupted his talk by galloping up to the two men. He clutched a blood-soaked bandanna to the left side of his head as he rode. McClintock noticed immediately that his revolver was missing from its holster, as was his rifle from its saddle scabbard.

Jack Harris climbed out of the saddle and walked up to Blake and McClintock a bit unsteadily. His mouth was shut tightly, and the cast in his left eye seemed more pronounced than ever. He seemed unable to speak. He turned the left side of his head toward them and lifted off the bandanna.

Blood was still trickling down and crusting on his left ear. A neat diamond shape was cut out of the high upper part of the ear.

"That's the Dunwell spread's earmark for cattle," Blake said, more surprised than sympathetic.

McClintock got to his feet. "I'll wash it for you."

"He wants you," Jake said.

"Who wants me?" Mournful John asked.

"El Caballito del Diablo. He's out there waiting for you. Alone."

"Come on." McClintock took Jake's arm. "I'll wash it for you."

"Hold on," Blake said. "I want to hear what happened."

"I was on my way here," Jake told him, "when I heard a calf bawl in that big thicket where the wagon trail bends toward town. I thought the calf might be sick or caught in something, so I went to look. That damn Injun jumped me from a hiding place and pulled me out of the saddle. It was he who'd imitated the calf and lured me there. He roped me while I was on the ground like you would a calf, bent my ear in two, and cut out a piece." He took a bloody diamond of ear cartilage out of a shirt pocket and looked at it sorrowfully on his palm. "Injun said he was sorry he didn't have a fire and a branding iron. Then he ran a finger along the edge of his knife blade and looked at my crotch. 'Pity I have to send you with a message or I'd fix you down there as well.' He'd have done it too. Then he caught my horse and sent me here. Told me he'd wait there for McClintock."

"I ain't a fool," McClintock said. "I ain't going."

"Damn you, you backshooting coward!" Blake screamed at him.

"Shut your mouth, you soft-handed fool," Mournful John said to him. "I ain't your servant. Never was."

"You swagger about like you're unbeatable," Blake taunted him. "Yet when a lone Indian ropes and earmarks one of your gunmen like a three-month-old calf, you're afraid to do anything about it."

"Watch your tongue," Mournful John said. "I've heard enough from you. I do as I please. For my own reasons. I explain to nobody."

"You don't have to," Blake shouted. "You're afraid. You're no bounty hunter. Just a backshooter. A drygulcher who runs when he's faced down by a lone Indian—"

Mournful John had been leading Jake away by the arm to the bunkhouse. He turned slowly around. His face was twisted in a mask of cold rage. Blake's voice faltered.

McClintock spoke in a low menacing tone. "Go for your gun."

Blake was so furious, he really believed at that moment that McClintock's nerve had cracked. If Blake could outdraw and kill this has-been, it would help make up for all he had been through. That's what he would do. Outdraw and kill this loathsome flimflam man.

Noah Blake's right hand dove for his gun. His fingers were still closing around the handle when McClintock's revolver barked. The .45 bullet whacked into the flesh of Blake's gut as if it were the succulent sap of a thick cactus.

Mournful John came back to stand over his victim, who lay writhing in agony on the ground. Blood ran though Blake's fingers where he clutched the bullet wound in his stomach, and low moaning came from his mouth.

Mournful John looked down at him for a while like he would at a fly caught in treacle.

"This ain't to put you out of your misery," he said

calmly to the writhing Blake as he pointed the barrel of his revolver down at his head. "I just ain't listening to that kind of talk from no man, and I'm making sure you ain't never going to talk again."

He squeezed the trigger, and the high-caliber bullet cracked apart Blake's skull to reveal a pulsating white membrane beneath the bone.

CHAPTER TWELVE

"The only witness was Jake Harris, and he told the sheriff that McClintock killed Blake in self-defense," Will Tucker informed Raider and Doc. "It remained a kind of standoff between the sheriff and Mournful John. I know Sheriff Dean would have liked to have taken him in, but he had no firm evidence, and he and his deputies were squared off against Mournful John and the two Harris brothers. I wouldn't have put my money on the side of law and order in that shoot-out. So the sheriff went back to town."

"Where's Mournful John now?" Doc asked.

"I don't know," Tucker replied. "Still at the Tumbling K, I guess."

"The sheriff should have ordered him off the spread at least."

"He didn't."

Doc looked thoughtful. "Sarah's there, and Blake's widow and children."

"I don't think McClintock would harm them," Raider

said. "He's too well known, and if word got out that he was harming women and children, no one would have him as a bounty hunter. No, McClintock won't be the one to harm them. The Harris brothers are the ones I'd worry about."

"They'll do what McClintock tells them," Tucker said.

"What if McClintock just rides off and leaves them there?" Doc asked.

"We gotta move all three of them off the Tumbling K," Raider said, determined.

Caballito laughed. "Let me go alone. When Mournful John sees me coming, he'll run away."

"Corner a rat and he'll fight back," Doc warned. "For the sake of the women and children, let's avoid a fight at the house. Let's drive them off the ranch first and then settle our differences with them."

There was general agreement on what needed to be done, but no agreement on how to do it. Whatever way they decided to go about things, they always came back to the same problem: How could any of them get near the Blake ranch buildings without starting a shooting war? The sheriff had to go out there again. That was the only answer.

Doc Weatherbee had to talk seriously with Judith several times before the mule would obey Sheriff Jackson Dean's commands. Even then, Doc had to call out every now and then to let Judith know he was on the wagon too, or else she stopped and could not be persuaded or frightened into moving forward again.

"I don't know why we have to use this contrary animal," Raider complained. "There must be dozens of agreeable mules in Williamville."

Doc explained to Caballito, who was also concealed with them in the back of the wagon, "Raider gets upset about Judith because he knows she's smarter than he is."

"Hell, she can't be that smart if she agrees to work for you," Raider put in.

Caballito decided to say nothing. He was not going to get himself in trouble by making personal remarks about a mule.

"There she goes again," Raider said, as the wagon lurched and they bounced their bones on the hard wood floor. "Any rock or hole that mule can find, she'll aim a wheel at it."

"Only when you're aboard," Doc observed drily.

"She's got the devil in her," was the sheriff's only comment.

As the wagon at length approached the buildings on the Tumbling K, Jake Harris walked out of the bunkhouse, rifle in hand.

"What can I do for you, Sheriff?" he called.

The sheriff looked at the little diamond cut out of the man's left ear and laughed openly. "You can't do nothing for me, Harris. Not now and not in the future neither."

"You looking for someone here?" Harris asked truculently.

"I came to talk with Mrs. Blake and it ain't none of your business."

"It *is* mine." Mournful John McClintock left the bunkhouse doorway and stood in the trail before the wagon so that Judith stopped when she came to him. "I was hired by her late husband to look after the family. That's what I aim to do."

Concealed in the back of the wagon, Doc put a hand on Caballito's shoulder to restrain him as they heard Mournful John's voice. He need not have done so. In the half darkness of their hiding place, he saw the Comanche's face—the face of a patient hunter who will not scare the quarry away by revealing his presence too soon. Doc heard Raider gently cursing to himself beneath a large piece of canvas. He too could be depended upon.

"If the Blakes hire you, that's their business," the sheriff was saying. "Now I also got my business, so if you'll kindly move out of my way—"

"Where are your deputies today, Sheriff?" McClintock asked in a playfully menacing way. "All alone, are you?"

"I got no reason to need reinforcements, way I see it," the sheriff said.

"What you got in that wagon? Why didn't you ride out on your horse?"

"I've no duty to answer any of your questions, except as plain civility in a public servant. You got that, McClintock? This is the last of your questions I'll answer, and then you'll get out of my way. I brought the wagon to offer Mrs. Blake and her children and their governess transportation into town if they needed it." The sheriff flicked the reins on the mule's rump. "G'yup there, Judith."

Judith didn't move.

"Seems like this here mule catches on faster than you do, Sheriff," Mournful John said, permitting himself a sardonic grin and reaching his hand out to pet Judith's nose.

Only McClintock's lightning-fast gunfighter's reactions saved him. The mule twisted her head sideways as his hand was about to rest on her nose, bared her enormous yellow teeth, and tried to chomp down on the fingers of his right hand, his gun hand. Mournful John literally pulled his fingers from between her closing teeth, leaving only a shirt cuff and part of a sleeve in her mouth.

Judith decided it was time to move on. Fast. Mournful John dodged out of the way as the mule came forward, and the wagon wheel missed him by inches. It was a good try on Judith's part.

Jake Harris guffawed, and Mournful John was too surprised to stop the sheriff now from reaching the Blake ranch house. Dean managed to persuade Judith to pull up real close to the house, so that the wagon's side was only a foot from its wall and the rear of the wagon was close to the far corner of the house. Doc, Raider, and Caballito were able to slip unseen around the side of the building as the sheriff went to the front door. They opened a window and climbed inside. From a room somewhere at the back, they could hear a piano playing and children's voices singing.

"She's in her bedroom," Sarah Cooper told them. "She's been hysterical on and off since her husband's death. I'm cooking and taking care of the children. The help in the house and most of the ranch hands have left. The ranch foreman and the few men those brutes haven't frightened off have to spend nearly all the daylight hours out on the range watching over the cattle."

The sheriff was polite but firm. "Mr. McClintock has just told me that he has been employed to protect the family. If you want him off the property, I'll have to hear that in person from Mrs. Blake. She's the proprietor now, and no one else will do."

"I'll see what I can do," Sarah said and left.

Doc said, "Well, at least McClintock and the Harrises hadn't attempted to get in the house."

"Yet," Raider added.

"You two are the only ones I've seen breaking in," the sheriff said, "and *I* helped you."

The sheriff said "you two" because he steadfastly refused to acknowledge the existence of the third, El Caballito del Diablo. Jackson Dean was as honest as a lawman is allowed to be, meaning he sometimes had to turn a blind eye. If Dean remained unaware of the presence of this Comanche fugitive, he could hardly be expected to arrest him. However, it was plain that the sheriff was less than happy with the arrangement.

Sarah came back, leading a haggard woman wrapped in a bedspread.

"Get them away from here," Mrs. Blake wailed, and for a moment Doc, Raider, and the others thought she was referring to them. "That man killed my dear husband, the finest man who ever set foot in Texas. Get him away from here. He and those other two should be put on trial for murder and hanged."

"Sorry to disturb you again, ma'am," Jackson Dean said. "I just had to hear it from your own mouth."

"My husband never hired that man to protect us. He paid him a bounty on rustlers. That's all. Now he and his two sidekicks won't leave till they've taken everything left to a defenseless woman and her young children."

She put her arm around the shoulders of a boy about seven, and Sarah held the hand of a girl maybe five.

"One last question, ma'am," the sheriff said. "Do you wish these two Pinkerton agents to assist you?"

Sarah spoke in a low rapid voice to Mrs. Blake, who seemed confused.

"Yes, by all means," Mrs. Blake finally said. "They can stay if they'll get rid of those three blackguards outside."

"With your permission I'll borrow a horse to ride back

to town.'' The sheriff turned to the others. ''All right, boys, I've done my part. Be sure to cover me with your rifles and make sure they don't follow me. And no shooting till after I'm gone. That way I'll just have to take your version of what happened.''

The sheriff opened the front door of the ranch house and stepped out. ''McClintock!''

Mournful John appeared at the bunkhouse door.

''The widder wants you off her property without delay.''

''I ain't leaving till I'm paid what I'm owed,'' Mournful John shouted back. ''She owes me five thousand dollars and the Harris brothers a thousand each. If she hasn't got the money, she'll have to pay us in livestock.''

''She owes you nothing,'' the sheriff said. ''You came here as a bounty hunter and that's how you'll leave.''

Mournful John ignored this and went back inside the bunkhouse.

Through the lace curtains on the windows, the three inside the ranch house watched the sheriff cross the open ground to the stables. Dean had brought a horse out into the open to saddle him when Ned Harris rode in with a packhorse loaded with provisions in tow. He had obviously just arrived from Williamville. Ned said nothing to the sheriff, but, curious, he just ran the two horses into the stable and went immediately wihtout unharnessing them to the bunkhouse.

The sheriff mounted the horse and rode off down the trail. While Raider and Caballito covered the departing lawman from the windows, Doc went to the back of the ranch house, through the kitchen, into a kind of yard where chickens scratched in the dirt and cats lay in the sun.

''Judith,'' Doc called in a low voice.

The mule came around the corner of the house with the wagon trundling after her. She cut the corner too sharp and the wagon wheel grazed the side of the house. Doc unhitched Judith, who drank from a trough of water and wandered off to eat some vegetables growing in a small garden.

Doc, Raider, and Caballito quieted the two children and persuaded Sarah to take them away from the front of the house. Blake's widow had again closeted herself in her room. McClintock and the Harrises couldn't leave without being seen by those inside the ranch house, but Doc and the others didn't have much hope they would try. They expected that fairly soon the three men would make a move on the house, which they thought undefended. The sheriff could be expected the next day with reinforcements. If McClintock and the Harrises were going to force money or livestock out of the widow, they were going to have to work on it soon. And they did.

Jake Harris stepped out of the bunkhouse, and his brother and Mournful John hung back at the door to watch him.

"We could take them all out with rifles right now," Raider muttered.

"That would be too kind to them," Caballito whispered back. "I have more interesting things planned for them."

Doc and Caballito stood on each side of the door, while Raider covered Jake's progress from the window.

"He's comin'."

They heard footsteps outside. A pause. They saw the inside door handle turn. The door pushed inward.

Caballito caught Jake by the throat and yanked him inside. Doc closed the door after him, without slamming it. Jake lay facedown on the floor, and his nose was bleeding. The Comanche was kneeling on his back, tying Jake's wrists behind his back with a rawhide thong. Caballito indicated a coiled lariat in a corner, and Doc brought it to him. He threaded the end of the lariat through the diamond-shaped hole cut in Jake's ear and tied a couple of half-knots at the end of the rope so it couldn't run back through the hole. Caballito removed Jake's sidearm, stood, and kicked Jake in the ribs till he stood also. Caballito led him to the door by the leash attached to his ear. Doc held the door open, and Caballito with a final well-placed kick propelled the unhappy gunman out into the open ground in front of the ranch house.

With his hands tied behind him, Jake staggered about at the end of the lariat as Caballito paid out more rope from inside the door and tied the end to the leg of a heavy armchair. When Jake reached as far as the rope allowed, he was reminded by a painful jerk in his left ear.

Ned Harris and Mournful John slipped inside the bunk-house door as they saw Jake emerge on the end of a rope. Jake warned them who was in the ranch house.

"We can't let them die without knowing who's killing them," Caballito said with satisfaction.

Although Doc had cooperated, there could be no doubt from the expression on his face that he regarded this incident with something less than approval. However, the grin on Raider's face signaled that he not only approved of it but was thoroughly enjoying it.

Jake Harris stood about at the end of the lariat and shouted to his brother and Mournful John. Rightly or wrongly, he had gotten the idea they were about to leave without him.

"Wait for me! Don't go!" he pulled on the lariat so that

his left ear stretched, and he twisted his hands desperately behind his back, trying to free them. "Wait for me."

"Him yelling like that at them is going to keep McClintock from thinking straight," Raider said.

"Don't bet on it," Doc answered.

Jake screamed, "Wait for me!"

He jerked his head so violently against the rope, that his ear split and the lariat fell free. Jake howled with pain and ran toward the stables. This was too much for Ned, who darted from the bunkhouse for the stables too, in order to free his brother's hands. Raider waited till Ned was around the corner of the bunkhouse and couldn't be covered by Mournful John's fire. Then he leaped through the ranch house window, shattering glass and delicate frames, to confront Ned Harris before he could reach his brother.

Neither man had his revolver drawn—Ned carried a .45 Colt Peacemaker and Raider his .44 Remington. It was only a question of who found his balance first, drew and cocked his gun, and pulled the trigger.

Raider had yanked his hat down over his eyes as he barreled through the glass. Although he had broken through with only some minor cuts, it took more time for him to recover from his great physical effort than it did for Ned Harris to halt his run and wheel about to face him. Ned's gun was leaving its holster while Raider was still getting his bearings and pushing his hat out of his eyes with his left hand. All the same, the fingers of Raider's right hand had gripped the wood-faced handle of his Remington and had begun to pull it from its holster. But later than Ned Harris . . .

Harris's gun flashed out. Raider let himelf fall backward, stretching his left hand behind to support his body. Ned Harris's slug passed well over his body. Raider's right knee was pointing at Harris, his gun was cocked, and he blew the bottom out of his holster. Raider could have sworn he felt the slug he had first fired travel alongside his right thigh and brush his knee as it sped toward Ned Harris.

His bullet hit Harris as the gunman was lowering his barrel for a second shot at Raider. The heavy lead slug spun the gaunt man's frame like a sheet of paper in a whirl of wind and slammed him against the timbered stable wall.

Ned Harris had given his life to save his brother, but that didn't mean Jake was going to stick around to witness Ned's last moments. Hands still bound behind him, he set off at a run around the stables toward the bunkhouse where McClintock was.

Raider ducked in behind Jake and used him as cover to get close to McClintock. Mournful John wasn't having this and lost no time in blasting Raider's cover out of the way—Jake hit the dust with a loud scream as McClintock's bullet tore into his innards.

Raider had time to get back to the cover of the stables. McClintock's slugs tore slivers from the wood boards on the corner by his head. Then Doc and Caballito's fire drove Mournful John back inside the bunkhouse doorway again, where he stood reloading his guns, determined Raider would not advance to take the bunkhouse by the rear or side.

They all saw him at the same time and held their fire— Noah Blake's son running from an open side window of the ranch house toward McClintock. The seven-year-old boy held his father's Colt .45 in both hands and manfully tried to raise its weight into a firing position as he ran.

CHAPTER THIRTEEN

The Colt went off and jumped out of the boy's grip. He clutched his right thumb for a moment and then stooped to pick up the weapon. His shot had gone wild, but there could be no doubt for whom it had been intended. His father's murderer. Mournful John McClintock.

The seven-year-old ran forward with the pistol held out before him again. The boy's plan was clear—he was going to run up to McClintock and shoot him at point-blank range, so that he couldn't miss even if his hands weren't strong enough to hold the gun steady. From the bunkhouse doorway, McClintock watched him come and slowly raised his pistol to take deliberate aim at the child.

"No! No! Don't!" Sarah Cooper ran like an antelope across the open ground behind the boy.

The boy hesitated and slowed at his governess's cries, and before he could get going again, she had knocked the Colt from his hands. Standing between him and McClintock, she pushed him back toward the ranch house.

Mournful John saw his opportunity and took it. Knowing that the presence of the woman and child would keep the others from firing for fear of hitting them, he ran from the bunkhouse doorway up behind Sarah and seized her with his left arm about her waist. Then he pressed the muzzle of his Colt into her neck and stood his ground.

"Raider, get away from the stables," McClintock shouted. "Take the boy back to the ranch house."

Raider holstered his pistol and stepped out of cover. He caught Blake's son by the arm and led him into the ranch house.

"Now you fellas listen and listen good," McClintock called to them from behind Sarah. "I'm taking this woman along to ensure my safe passage. I'll release her unharmed along the way. We're going to saddle up and take that packhorse. You take a shot at me and she gets it."

He pulled her inside the bunkhouse, and in a short while she reappeared carrying his saddlebags and bedroll. McClintock walked behind her, keeping his hands free. Five minutes later they rode away. They had about three hours before sundown.

They tried not to move a muscle as Caballito listened in the darkness. At first he thought he heard the sounds of three horses moving. Then he was less sure. Now he heard nothing.

Mournful John McClintock had set off south across the level ranges. He was still on Tumbling K property when darkness fell. There was not much brush here on the level land, so that it was possible to travel by the light of the stars.

"If we keep heading south," Doc said, "we take a big risk. McClintock might stop anyplace and change direction or even loop back. Right now we know he passed this way. I say we stop here for the night and follow his tracks in the morning. He has an unwilling companion and that packhorse, so he'll be slowed down. We can catch him.''

For want of any better suggestions, the others agreed. They spent a chilly night without food on the dusty ground and were happy to start moving again in the half-light before dawn.

"They traveled here without being able to see where they were going," Caballito said, pointing to their tracks. "Look, the horses couldn't see this gully until they stepped into it, and look here and here at the deep prints where they lost their balance.''

It was soon evident that McClintock had not stopped for the night, but had relentlessly pushed south through the darkness.

Water was hard to find. Their great thirst kept their minds off their hunger, and they pushed on, following the tracks. The open range country gave way to brush country, the *brasada*. Huge thickets of thorn bushes were everywhere, hiding cattle, wild pig, turkeys, and blue quail. Cicadas rattled as the sun warmed them—and so too did the coiled snakes when their horses came too close. Now and then they came unexpectedly on streams running in high-walled gullies through the otherwise parched land. The water was undrinkable for humans, and even the horses drank sparingly.

The sun was now high over their heads, and everything shimmered in waves of almost unbearable heat. The gray soil stretched away as far as the eye could see, and its gray dust had coated the leaves of the thorn scrub so that all the grayness blended in with the white haze of heat in the sky.

"They have to stop sometime," Cabalitto said. "Then we will catch up.''

"Not if they can keep going until darkness," Doc said. "Then we'll lose them again."

Caballito shook his head. "He couldn't keep that up. No, you'll see very shortly where he is headed."

Caballito was right. Unexpectedly they came out of the brush onto the bank of a shallow, medium-sized river.

"The Rio Grande," Caballito announced.

Two minutes later they were in Mexico and again following the tracks.

"He still has Sarah captive," Caballito said. "I would have noticed the difference in the prints the hooves make if she was not on that horse. I had expected he would let her go north of the river. I think he believes Pinkerton agents will not enter Mexico without clearance."

"I didn't see any notices saying this was Mexico," Doc said.

"Looks like Texas to me," Raider agreed.

"Soon now Mournful John must rest," Caballito said, looking at the tracks with certainty.

It didn't stay looking like Texas for very long. The thorny thickets gave way to cactus and the gray soil to desert sand. Here streams were just meandering lines of liquid mud, with occasional willows, cottonwoods, and rank grass along their banks. Elsewhere only isolated clumps of sagebrush, greasewood, and mesquite grew, apart from cactus.

The tracks were easy to follow, and now they looked anxiously ahead for a sign of the dust cloud three horses would raise. They saw nothing but more and more land shimmering in waves of heat. There was no escape from the sun here. Beneath anything that offered the least bit of shade, resident rattlesnakes buzzed their warnings.

They came across a lone Indian man walking purposefully somewhere into the empty desert. No, he had not seen the horses that had made these tracks, he told Caballito in Spanish. He directed them to his village, which McClintock had missed. The village was a collection of flat-roofed adobe houses surrounded by plots of beans, corn, peas, and melons. They paused only long enough to buy food and fill their containers with drinking water, then they retraced their steps into the desolate landscape and set out on McClintock's trail once again.

"She doesn't speak any Spanish or English," Caballito said of the wrinkled old Indian woman they found by the deserted church.

He continued talking to her in what Doc and Raider assumed was the Comanche language—some of which seemed to be understood by the old woman.

After a while Caballito turned to the others. "The tracks lead here and then go on, so we know they have been here. I don't think this old woman was fully aware they were here. She keeps on saying that we must see this church that she is looking after till the padres return."

Doc smiled. "All right. Let's do what she says."

The outside of the church resembled other old Spanish mission churches. Inside it was wrecked. Everything of value had been looted long ago, hands and noses had been broken off lifesize wooden statues, bullet holes pocked dark canvases of emaciated saintly monks, initials and names were carved in wood or scored in the walls, mutilating frescoes and murals, shattered stained glass littered the floor.

"Apaches?" Raider asked.

"Some of them," Caballito said. He pointed to the names on the walls. "But these men were not Apaches."

Raider and Doc read the names: Wilson, Davenport,

Hewlett . . . Apaches don't leave signatures on walls, and not too many of them have adopted names like those. The dates all fell in one year—1849.

"This must have been one of the routes to California in the gold rush," Doc said. "I suppose this is what the old woman remembers and is still hoping the priests will come back."

They went outside again, and Doc gave the old lady a silver dollar and gestured his thanks for the tour of the church. Caballito spoke to her again and reported that she was even less informative than before, insisting that they visit another old ruin.

"She called it Rancho San Miguel?" Doc asked. "Maybe that's where she thinks McClintock has gone."

Caballito asked her this but could not make sense out of what she told him.

The sandy earth on the way to the ranch was covered with cholla and prickly pear. Here and there organ-pipe cactus stood out, and giant columns of saguaro cactus rose nearly forty feet in the air with a circumference of more than ten feet.

They climbed up a rise toward the ruins. Everything had been built of stone, and they looked about them at the arcades, courtyards, fountains, and ornamental gardens— all now ruined beyond repair.

Raider said, "These people in Rancho San Miguel lived in higher style than the Texas ranchers we've seen."

Fire-blackened stone walls around roofless rooms stood as mute evidence to what had happened here. Three horses grazed in a shaded, broken-down courtyard.

Raider and Caballito sprang from their horses and disappeared among the ravaged walls, leaving Doc holding the three mounts. He was annoyed at this but realized he had better get the three horses to safety. He led them some distance away and tethered them in the shade. He pulled Raider and Caballito's rifles from their saddles and carried them with his own. The sun was getting low in the sky, and the day's heat was beginning to let up.

Doc was on his way back to the ruined hacienda when he suddenly came across McClintock and Sarah. McClintock forced Sarah down behind some rocks, and Doc dove for cover behind a small sand hill. Doc opened fire with his rifle right away to alert Raider and Caballito.

When Mournful John tried to use Sarah as a shield again, she pulled away from him and ran a few paces, then fell. Doc stopped McClintock from following her by peppering the area with bullets.

When he used up the magazine in his own rifle, he switched to Raider's carbine to keep McClintock pinned down while he reloaded his own weapon. There was no way he could hit McClintock behind the cover of those rocks. Sarah was vulnerable to him anytime he decided to use her. Meanwhile he was firing back at Doc from the better shooting position.

While firing to keep McClintock's head down and waiting for the others to arrive, Doc noticed he was hitting the base of a giant saguaro, almost thirty feet high, with longitudinal ridges like a Greek temple column. Doc thought of the pulpy cactus flesh that was soft in the middle and held itself up by the pressure of its sap against its hard rind.

He blasted away at the base in a straight line across it. His ammunition fitted Caballito's rifle but not Raider's carbine, so he used the carbine sparingly to keep Mournful John in place as he reloaded the other two guns. He emptied them again into the base of the monster cactus.

McClintock ignored what he regarded as wild shooting over his head and never bothered to look where the bullets were going.

Doc had seen lumberjacks fell big trees and was aware of the brief pause when the huge trunk begins to topple and the men have time to clear away before it falls.

The saguaro gave no such warning. One moment it stood there, and the next, a two-ton column of watery green pulp came crashing down.

Doc ran forward. Mournful John McClintock lay under the huge plant, squashed like a lizard under a wagon wheel.

After a big meal from the provisions brought by the packhorse, Doc and Sarah retreated to a private enclave in the ruined hacienda.

"Why are Raider and Caballito mad at you?" Sarah asked.

"They're a little sore at me because I got McClintock, not them. Also because of the way I got him. You heard Raider call it Yankee trickery."

She laughed. "What do Yankees know about cactuses?"

They cuddled beneath blankets under a starry sky. Doc's mouth was too busy to answer the lady's question.

JAKE LOGAN

___	0-872-16823	**SLOCUM'S CODE**	$1.95
___	0-867-21071	**SLOCUM'S DEBT**	$1.95
___	0-872-16867	**SLOCUM'S FIRE**	$1.95
___	0-872-16856	**SLOCUM'S FLAG**	$1.95
___	0-867-21015	**SLOCUM'S GAMBLE**	$1.95
___	0-867-21090	**SLOCUM'S GOLD**	$1.95
___	0-872-16841	**SLOCUM'S GRAVE**	$1.95
___	0-867-21023	**SLOCUM'S HELL**	$1.95
___	0-872-16764	**SLOCUM'S RAGE**	$1.95
___	0-867-21087	**SLOCUM'S REVENGE**	$1.95
___	0-872-16927	**SLOCUM'S RUN**	$1.95
___	0-872-16936	**SLOCUM'S SLAUGHTER**	$1.95
___	0-867-21163	**SLOCUM'S WOMAN**	$1.95
___	0-872-16864	**WHITE HELL**	$1.95
___	0-425-05998-7	**SLOCUM'S DRIVE**	$2.25
___	0-425-06139-6	**THE JACKSON HOLE TROUBLE**	$2.25
___	0-425-06330-5	**NEBRASKA BURNOUT #56**	$2.25
___	0-425-06338-0	**SLOCUM AND THE CATTLE QUEEN #57**	$2.25
___	06381-X	**SLOCUM'S WOMEN #58**	$2.25
___	06532-4	**SLOCUM'S COMMAND #59**	$2.25
___	06413-1	**SLOCUM GETS EVEN #60**	$2.25

Available at your local bookstore or return this form to:

B **BERKLEY**
Book Mailing Service
P.O. Box 690, Rockville Centre, NY 11571

Please send me the titles checked above. I enclose _____ Include 75¢ for postage and handling if one book is ordered; 25¢ per book for two or more not to exceed $1.75. California, Illinois, New York and Tennessee residents please add sales tax.

NAME _____

ADDRESS _____

CITY _____ STATE/ZIP _____

(allow six weeks for delivery)

162b